THE MONTCHERRY MURDER

A LEGAL THRILLER

ANANYAA BAHADUR
'BEVIBINN'

AMARYLLIS

AMARYLLIS

An imprint of Manjul Publishing House Pvt. Ltd.
• C-16, Sector 3, Noida, Uttar Pradesh 201301, India
Website: www.manjulindia.com
Registered Office:
• 10, Nishat Colony, Bhopal 462 003 – India
Distribution Centres
Ahmedabad, Bengaluru, Bhopal, Chennai, Hyderabad,
Kolkata, Mumbai, Noida, Pune

The Montcherry Murder by Ananyaa Bahadur

This edition first published in India in 2023

ISBN 978-93-5543-332-9

Cover design: Misha Oberoi

Printed and bound in India by Thomson Press (India) Ltd.

Contents

Chapter 1

The Cruise

On a beautiful moonlit night in the Hamptons, a fine dining cruise sailed, carrying the rich and the elite for a private dinner. The cruise had the finest food, exotic drinks, impeccable service, and a plush ambience. Seated at the best table were Ethan, his best friend Timothy, and their new friend, Jasper. They were enjoying the magnificent view of the vast ocean with the cool breeze blowing onto their faces, ruffling their impeccably-kept hair. It was not just dinner, but an experience.

Their table drew a lot of attention, particularly from those of the opposite gender, who could not resist the good looks of the renowned attorney, Ethan Carson. Their eyes were glued to his strong jawline, deep brown eyes, and sun-kissed skin. The acclaimed lawyer was immaculately dressed in a black suit with a chic tie that screamed sophistication. Ethan was a total charm with an amazing style. He was well aware of his alluring personality and often used it to his advantage.

They were making some decent small talk when they heard the gruff voice of their host, Mr. Park, over the microphone. “Good evening, my dear friends! Thank you for coming and celebrating my phenomenal win in court with me! I am elated that I am here on this cruise with you and not rotting in some prison cell.” There was laughter and a huge round of applause from his guests. Mr. Park made a gesture to quieten his friends and continued. “It wouldn't have been possible without my superhero attorney here, Mr. Ethan Carson.” He raised his glass in the direction of Ethan and roared, “Let's raise a toast to the star of the evening!”

Guests turned to face Ethan as they hooted and clapped. Ethan stood up and raised his glass to acknowledge their appreciation, his six-foot-tall frame and smile mesmerizing everyone around. He briefly bowed with grace and sat down as the cheering faded, settling the locks of his brown hair that fell over his face.

The party continued with glitz and glamour as the night progressed. Exactly at midnight, there was a loud squeal of delight. Everyone's focus shifted to the source of the sound as a group of waiters, along with the head chef, wheeled in a lavish three-tier cake to a table and then discreetly stood aside. Once again, Mr. Park took to the microphone. “Friends, tonight also happens to be the birthday of my very special older sister here. Happy birthday to my darling, Sheryl. Let us all celebrate together and shower her with our wishes.”

The guests gathered around the table, where the woman and her children sat. Everyone sang the birthday song with complete vigor as Sheryl cut the cake. The waiters trolleyed the cake away, for it to be served later. As guests were returning to their tables, the cruise entertainers began an exotic dance performance. The guests cheered enthusiastically; this party was not getting over any time soon.

"Birthdays always manage to remind me of how old I'm getting," shrugged Timothy, loosening the red tie that he had worn to match his Persian blue suit. The moonlight fell faintly but visibly onto his light brown eyes as he looked at Ethan and Jasper.

"Yeah, makes us realize we aren't gonna live forever," smirked Ethan.

"Ethan, you're talking as if you are an old man who does nothing but... uh... reads books in a nursing home," said Jasper and chuckled at his own joke.

Ethan eyed the formally dressed Jasper affectionately as he took in his pitch-black suit and ultramarine blue tie. He could tell that Jasper was uncomfortable in the suit but was trying his best to not show it.

Ethan's lips curved into a suppressed grin, as he recollected how Jasper had laughed at the suggestion of wearing a suit to the formal dinner. Jasper had retaliated, "Are you kiddin' me, dude?! Just imagine, a purple-haired guy tryin' to pull off a formal suit! Doesn't go with my image, man!"

However, Ethan didn't budge. "Trust me, Jasper, you would feel out of place in your leather jacket and ripped jeans at the party. Just wear the suit once, for my sake."

Jasper had immense respect and affection for Ethan

and eventually gave in. "Okay, buddy. Only for you, man. I think I might have a suit lying around somewhere."

Within a short duration, Ethan had taken a liking to his fun-loving neighbor, Jasper. He had recently moved into the villa adjoining Ethan's at the Hamptons. When Mr. Park had insisted that Ethan bring his friends to the party and have a good time, he had invited Timothy and Jasper.

The three friends were enjoying the music and were chatting casually. "You're one of the world's most renowned criminal lawyers, Ethan. You've never lost a case in your whole damn life! Quite an accomplishment, considering you are so young," stated Jasper.

"Young?! No, I'm 34 years old. No way is that young," laughed Ethan.

"34?! You don't look a day over 23! What's your secret, buddy? I'm 28 myself and as compared to you, I look ancient!" said Jasper, clearly in awe of Ethan.

"C'mon, man. Thanks for the compliment," smiled Ethan, his tone reflecting a hint of pride.

Timothy smirked. "Don't play at being modest, Ethan. You literally have over 8 million followers on social media. It's not even fair that you have so many followers when you aren't even that active."

Jasper laughed and gave a high five to Timothy in agreement as Ethan playfully smacked Timothy on the back.

Just then, Jasper got a call and excused himself.

He returned soon and said, "Guys, sorry to be

the party spoiler. My folks just called. They have made sudden plans to visit me tomorrow and will be arriving here early in the morning. I haven't seen them in months, and it's the first time they are coming to this new home of mine. If I have to be up to greet them early tomorrow, I'll have to leave now."

Ethan replied, "Yes, of course! I guess we can request Mr. Park to make the required arrangements."

They scanned the place for their flamboyant host. They found Mr. Park sitting with his friends, jiving to some live music. Ethan politely interrupted him and said, "It's a great party, Mr. Park!"

Mr. Park grinned and said, "The credit goes to you, Mr. Carson! Without your expertise, I would have been doomed!"

Ethan gave him a warm smile and said, "Always at your service, Mr. Park. My friend here needs to get back to the shore. Would it be possible to arrange for a speedboat?"

Mr. Park responded, looking at Jasper, "Oh sure! Hope you had a good time, young man."

Jasper nodded with a smile, "Absolutely, sir! Thank you for having me over."

They all headed towards the lower deck, where Mr. Park instructed the crew to see to the arrangements. The crew led Jasper to the speedboat for his journey back. Mr. Park wished Ethan and Timothy well. "Enjoy the party, you two. I will see you in a while." he then added with a wink, "Have to massage some egos and shake some hands."

Ethan and Timothy chuckled and replied, "Sure, we are good. Please go ahead."

There were hardly any people on the lower deck. As they watched Jasper leave, Timothy tapped his fingers restlessly on the railing and mumbled, "I envy those who grew up with parents and were fortunate to have a loving home."

Ethan tried to evade the topic, as it touched a nerve. His gaze landed on Timothy's finger rings as the moonlight made the gems shine. Gesturing towards the rings, Ethan muttered, "Timothy Ann, you still wear these! Are you still just as superstitious? You have come a long way from the disaster you had got yourself into. You don't need these rings now."

Timothy had a faraway look as he gazed at the deep dark waters while brooding over past events in his life. The breeze felt soothing as they stood on the deck. The gentle lashing of the waves filled in the silence that hung between them. Timothy sighed, "Sometimes, life amazes me with the twists and turns it takes. Come to think of it, if you didn't lose your parents in that car accident, and if you didn't have to change multiple foster homes due to some issue or the other, we wouldn't even have met." He patted Ethan fondly and said, "At least you know who your parents were. I don't even know who threw me in the orphanage."

"Yeah, I was still a kid when my world shattered due to the sudden death of my parents," said Ethan in a low voice. "Being an only child and having no extended family, I had no one to call my own. However, meeting you gave me a sense of belonging. You became the brother I never had."

Suddenly, Ethan started laughing, as he recalled a particular incident. "Remember when you told me to shove food down my pockets so that you could feed your hungry 'guinea pig', which was actually a rat that you had found on the street?" That made Timothy grin as he remembered his antics.

However, the next moment, a thought wiped the grin off Timothy's face and he said, "Well, soon after that, everything started going downhill for me. Don't know when I got friendly with that man who lured me into dealing drugs. I used to go to the given location with a briefcase full of drugs and would come back with one full of cash. All that mattered to me then was the 100 dollars he gave me for each deal. After being kicked out of our foster home on being caught, I felt that I had all the freedom to be as I pleased and continued in the drug business. Though I made a lot of money, it was too late by the time I realized that I had thrown my life away." His voice had gone hoarse, choked with the emotional turmoil that he always experienced each time he went down memory lane of his dark past.

"After you were caught by the foster parents and had to leave, I missed you a lot, buddy. We did not see each other for so many years," recalled Ethan.

"Yeah well, we went our separate ways. My only regret in life then was losing touch with you, which is why, years later, when I thought that my life was over, I could think of no one else but my long-lost brother. I was caught dealing drugs and was charged with that huge criminal case. I am so glad I looked you up and got in touch. I still remember how shocked I was when you told me that you had gone to Harvard and had become a lawyer!" exclaimed Timothy.

"Well, the day you left the orphanage, I realized that life was not going to be a bed of roses for people like us. I became determined to put in all my efforts into becoming capable of earning a good living. I was suddenly moved again to a new foster home. The new family was a believer in education and encouraged me to focus on academics. It all paid off when I got the scholarship to study law at Harvard." Ethan smiled, proud of his hard work and achievements.

"If not for you, Ethan, I would still be rotting behind bars," said Timothy. A shiver ran down his spine as he thought about those difficult times.

"Oh, Timothy! I was more than happy to help out my only brother in the world. It was the least I could do. I had to take the case." explained Ethan.

"Then you did what you do best. You won!" said Timothy, with a smile.

Timothy recollected how Ethan had refused to accept any fees for fighting the case for him, calling it drug money. As his payment, Ethan had asked him to quit drugs and work towards getting a respectable job.

Ethan interrupted his thoughts as he said, "Well, look where we are now. Who could have thought then that one day you would be an honorable doctor in one of the most renowned hospitals in town? In fact, I trust your medical input on my cases so much that I've made you accompany me to court so many times. The way you turned your life around is absolutely commendable," Ethan put a hand on Timothy's shoulder. "I am glad you left your dark past behind." He had got a degree, got married, had children, and now lived a peaceful life.

Timothy nodded in acknowledgment. He glanced at the rings on his fingers, and joked, "Ethan, now to answer your initial question, if these gems help me keep sane, then why the hell not?!" Ethan smiled and gave in.

A wave dashed against the ship, making a bit of a splash. The sudden sound of the wave jolted Timothy out of his gloom. He turned to face Ethan and apologized. "Sorry, bro! We've come to have a good time at this party, and I took you on an emotional trip. When Jasper mentioned his parents, it triggered my childhood memories."

Ethan shook his head and said empathetically, "That's all right, brother. We have gone through a lot to be here today! Also, it's one hell of a story now, isn't it?"

Timothy laughed in agreement. "C'mon! Let's go back to the party and get a drink."

They got their drinks and sat back at their table. Timothy raised his glass and said, "Cheers to our friendship!"

"Cheers!" smiled Ethan, raising his glass.

After a while, they decided to head back. They returned to the shore and were greeted by Ethan's driver, who drove them home. The party was still rocking. The two friends crashed at Ethan's weekend home, a huge sea-facing villa in the Hamptons.

Chapter 2

Ethan Carson

"Good morning, my love," said a warm voice. Ethan opened his eyes to his most cherished sight, the face of his beautiful wife, Sienna.

"Good morning, darlin'. I saw you up in the study, engrossed in your work, when I returned from the party this morning. Did you get any sleep at all?" asked Ethan, his voice still hoarse.

"I just finished writing another chapter of my new book, *Lights out*. I'll try and catch some sleep in the afternoon." She nudged him to get up and continued, "I'm hungry. Come on, let's eat something."

They freshened up and moved out to the patio, their favorite place in the villa, where breakfast had been laid out. It overlooked the manicured gardens and the beautiful ocean beyond.

Their butler came in and informed them, "Sir, Mr. Ann had an early breakfast and has left for the city. He asked me to tell you that he did not want to wake you up, so he left without meeting you."

Ethan nodded and asked him to get some freshly brewed coffee. They enjoyed their breakfast, after which, the couple went back to their weekend villa routine. Sienna's canvas and easel were set up on one side of the patio, whereas Ethan's favorite recliner was placed on the other side. Sienna painted, losing herself in her world of colors, while Ethan read his case files.

The serene setting was interrupted by the sound of footsteps going from their private gate to the beach. Ethan loved having this private access to the beach. He looked up fondly towards the gate in anticipation.

In a few seconds, Evan and Alexi, their two children, aged 6 and 8 respectively, ran in with their nanny behind them.

"Look, Dad! We collected so many shells," exclaimed Evan.

Ethan hugged his dear kids as they settled down beside him on his large recliner. He then helped them count and sort their treasures from the beach.

Meanwhile, Evan, the younger of the two and the more curious one, observed his mother engrossed in her painting. He commented, "Mom, you are an awesome painter! Makes me wonder if you are a writer or a painter."

Ethan chuckled and replied, "Well, my lil' boy, your mom is multi-talented."

Sienna turned towards him, and they exchanged a loving look.

However, Evan was ready with his next question. "Dad, how did you meet Mom?"

Alexi rolled her eyes and said, "Evan! Don't you get tired of asking the same question? You must've asked it, like, a million times already!"

"No way! Mom, ask Alexi not to butt in," complained Evan.

Sienna gave a stern look. Evan knew what it meant and immediately apologized. "Okay, okay. Sorry, Alexi." Then he turned towards his father and looked at him curiously.

Ethan knew Evan wouldn't budge. He smiled as he narrated the story for the umpteenth time, though with just as much enthusiasm as always. "You know, I am a big fan of mystery novels. They were my constant companions growing up. One day, while I was returning home from court, I read about a book signing event featuring your mom, the bestselling author, at a bookstore in my neighborhood. I had been intrigued by her earlier novel, which was also a bestseller. I decided to be there, and we liked each other instantly." He said all this while gazing at Sienna, recalling how they had fallen in love at first sight. "We kept meeting each other thereafter and got married around six months later."

"Happy?" Ethan grinned and looked at both his kids, who were listening in rapt silence, as if it was their favorite Disney story. They snapped out of their thoughts as Ethan announced, "Now children, get ready. Your teacher will be here within the hour."

"Why can't we go to a normal school, Dad? I hate home schooling," said Alexi with a frown.

"You know we can't send you to regular school, kids. You both are way ahead of your age groups," explained

Sienna in an exasperated tone, having answered this question many times before.

Alexi and Evan were much smarter than most children their age. Hence, they were home-schooled by teachers who visited their home and taught them at their pace. They had the knowledge of an average 10- or 12-year-old.

"Yes, my dear, you will find regular school slow-paced. Today, a professor from Yale is coming to talk to you about the basics of law. He is a dear friend and is very excited to meet you both," explained Ethan. He took a keen interest in his children's education and hired the best teachers from all fields to give them a holistic educational experience.

"Law! Now we will know all about your work, Dad," said Evan with excitement.

They ran off for a quick swim at their rooftop pool before getting ready for the professor. Ethan loved to work from his villa in the Hamptons during the weekend while relaxing with his family, unless he was in the middle of a tough trial.

After the professor left, Ethan excitedly had a rich discussion about law with his little kids. At moments like these, Ethan felt reassured about his decision of home schooling his children.

Sunday evening was a routine return for the whole family to their home in New York City. The kids' home schooling, therefore, fitted in perfectly well with their lifestyle. The Carson family enjoyed the drive back to their city life after a late, relaxed lunch by the pool.

The next morning, Ethan felt elated as he sat in his office, geared to win the world. His office had one of the best views in Manhattan. It was on the top floor of the tallest, plushest high-rise in the heart of New York. The skyscrapers were beneath him. He felt like the king, and pictured the buildings below him as his kingdom.

He was a senior partner in the firm Bennett International. The firm occupied the top four floors of the building.

Given a choice, almost every convict in the country would pick him as their lawyer. However, being at the top of his game, his fee was too steep for anyone but the elite. Therefore, his clientele included only millionaires and celebrities.

He was the only one of his kind, and he believed that nobody could ever beat him, until…now.

Chapter 3

The New Murder Case

"Ethan, you have to take this case. THE Liam Montcherry wants to sign with us and will give us his diamond business account if we win this murder case for him. This would bring huge business to the firm," announced Michelle Bennett, the managing partner of the firm, as she stepped into Ethan's cabin. Michelle was in her early forties. She was divorced and had dedicated her life to her firm.

"Sounds exciting," replied Ethan.

Michelle began explaining the case. "Liam Montcherry is being accused of his wife's murder on their first wedding anniversary. The story goes like this… On their first wedding anniversary, Liam's wife, Cloe Montcherry, was—"

At this point, Ethan interrupted Michelle. "—found dead in their house. Liam had pleaded 'not guilty'. He had been taken into custody but was later released on bail. Based on evidence presented by the prosecution during the preliminary hearing, the court had found probable cause to hold this over for trial. Liam Montcherry was so furious at his defense lawyers that he fired them in the court itself, just after the hearing. Right!?" Ethan was visibly proud of himself.

"You've heard," stated Michelle in a controlled, yet annoyed voice.

"Michelle, the whole of New York has heard. It's all over the news on every channel out there," informed Ethan.

"All right, then. We are his new Defense. Make sure we don't get fired as well. Jury selection is to begin in a week. I'll email the files to you. Keep me updated," said Michelle with a smile and walked out. Ethan and Michelle had a fantastic working relationship and had immense respect for each other.

Ethan pulled out a soda from his fridge to keep himself hydrated while working. He had a mini-fridge and a coffee machine strategically placed close to his desk, making them easily accessible. He could never compromise on his perfect cup of coffee and hence preferred to make his own. His files and notebooks were placed in a wooden cabinet right next to the shelf which had a dozen mystery novels. He liked to read novels in his free time, but little did he know that starting today, free time was going to be a luxury he would seldom experience.

He walked towards the large desk that dominated his office and settled into his leather chair, waiting for the email from Michelle. Three laptops were placed perfectly on the desk, to make his work more efficient. He was almost obsessive about his work and preferred doing his own research. He observed the minutest of details that others would often ignore or consider irrelevant. This had also helped him stay on top of his game.

As soon as he received Michelle's email with all the details, he got to work. He opened up his email on the side laptop and a browser on the center laptop to look up anyone or anything when needed, and he kept the third laptop on the other side open to view the crime scene documents.

Ethan was unable to examine the crime scene physically, as it had been a week since the murder, and the forensic work was already complete. He did his best to find his way around the case files. There were various pictures in the case file. The victim's body was found on her bed with a pillow left on her face. Some pictures, therefore, did not reveal her face. The forensic team had later removed the pillow during their examination. Hence, there were also some clear pictures of the victim's face.

Ethan pondered over various aspects of what appeared to be the simplest crime scene of his career. 'Something just isn't right. A crime scene being so clean is hardly ever natural,' Ethan thought to himself.

"It seems like someone had killed her by suffocating her with a pillow. She must have been asleep at the time, as no signs of physical harm like scratches, cuts, or bruises were found on her body," said Ethan aloud to himself. However, Cloe's phone was found in shattered pieces besides her bed.

"There could be two logical reasons for this... Either there was some struggle between the killer and the victim, and the phone got smashed, or the killer did not want anyone to see her phone's contents and destroyed it on purpose." Ethan continued speaking his thoughts aloud, still alone in the room.

Other than the broken phone and the pillow, the room seemed to be in perfect order. Liam was the last person to have seen her alive.

The sudden ringing of Ethan's phone sprung him out of his thoughts. It was Michelle. She said, "Ethan, ignore the current autopsy results, as they are now inadmissible in court."

"Why is that? I have already started working with that as a base!" said Ethan, frustrated at the unexpected hurdle.

"Well, Ethan, look closely. It was done by Timothy Ann. It appears that the whole world is aware of your deep friendship with him. The prosecutor did not accept the autopsy results as there is a conflict of interest with Timothy being your friend, now that we are taking the case. The prosecution has now requested a neutral party to re-examine the results and provide a fresh report. The autopsy by the new medical examiner should start soon, and the results should come within 10 days," explained Michelle.

"Damn! How did I miss that? This just delays things for everyone. I do trust Timothy's medical skills, though, and I am sure the results will come back the same. I will wait for the new report to talk about it in court," said Ethan. He hung up.

He needed to work on getting more information to make a tight case. He called up his associate, Martin Diaz. "Martin, where are you? I haven't seen you all morning. We've got a case."

"Yeah, yeah, I'm on my way. Something came up," said Martin.

Ethan was annoyed. *"You're still not at work?!"*

"Yeah, I know I'm late. I'm sorry, I'm on my way," replied an out-of-breath Martin.

Martin had just passed out of Harvard Law and had always been in awe of Ethan. It was his dream to work at Bennet International. Getting to work for Ethan as an associate was just the icing on the cake for him.

After 10-15 minutes, Martin rushed into Ethan's office and apologized. "Hey, sorry I'm late. I was stuck in traffic."

"It's all right for now. Anyway we've got Liam Montcherry's wife's murder case. I'm sure you've heard about it. We needa defend Liam," informed Ethan.

"Well, I haven't heard the details, though I'm aware that Liam is a business tycoon who deals with gems and diamonds. I know that his wife has been murdered, but apart from that, nothing much," shrugged Martin.

"Okay, then. Here's some background information for you. Liam is a billionaire and had a net worth of 50 billion dollars at one point. Liam was at the extreme top of his career then. He is most known for selling diamonds and has celebrities and millionaires as his clientele. He has numerous assets and stakes in various companies. His company, Montcherry Luxury, has a net worth of millions of dollars. All the celebs who can afford to buy diamonds, only buy them from him, and whoever wears one is royalty to the rest of the world." elaborated Ethan.

"What do you mean, 'had' a net worth of 50 billion dollars? Did he get robbed or something?" asked Martin, raising his brows.

"Well, not exactly robbed. He is one of those guys who couldn't handle money. He lost over 8 billion dollars recently, when he got hooked on gambling and got addicted. He lost a lot of what he had," informed Ethan.

"Hmmm, feel kind of bad for him. Now he lost his wife as well," murmured an empathetic Martin.

"All right, good soul. Now about his wife and their not-so-peaceful married life. His wedding to Cloe was the talk of the town. They had a courtship of eight months before Liam had popped the question in style. They looked madly in love and were the paparazzi's favorite couple. They attended all the events together, always dressed to impress with matched outfits, and kept their social media accounts buzzing with their PDA moments. However, lately, after Liam's gambling losses, the paparazzi had caught and published some of their not-so-romantic pictures," elaborated Ethan.

"Yes, a picture of them yelling at each other with annoyed faces, actually became the local template for several memes. I remember seeing this on Facebook. The couple had tried to make up for it by leaking some romantic holiday pictures where they both looked happy and in love. It's another story that It backfired, and became a 'before versus after' meme. All in all, the couple kept the media houses happy," said Martin as they both shared a laugh.

"Well, coming back to the case, Ethan, would you know if Cloe had any enemies at her workplace? Maybe someone met her on the night of the murder. What was her line of work, anyway?" inquired Martin.

"Cloe was a fashion designer and had her own line of clothing. After they got married, she collaborated with Liam's company, Montcherry Luxury. Their collaboration was a huge hit and brought them immense fame and success. She was known to be shrewd with her business dealings. None of her secretaries lasted for more than a week due to her arrogant attitude. Being one of the best in her business brought her a lot of competition. She was known to go to any extreme to be ahead of her competitors. Therefore, she made many enemies as she progressed in her career. I checked up on a few of 'em. Unfortunately, none of them were anywhere near her on the night of the murder," informed Ethan.

"In that case, Ethan, looks like we need to find an alibi for Liam," said Martin.

The jury selection was to begin on Tuesday, which gave Ethan exactly a week to prepare his case to win. He was the defense lawyer, hence his job was to plead Liam 'not guilty'. Ethan knew he could win this case. He only needed to find the right witnesses, proper evidence, and a tight alibi for Liam at the estimated time of the murder. His first objective was to find out if it was indeed Liam who had murdered his wife.

Ethan had multiple meetings with Liam during

the next few days. Liam always looked heartbroken. He went through Liam's alibi over and over with him. Ethan was not completely convinced, but realized that he had no choice but to take Liam at face value.

During one of their meetings, Ethan inquired, "How was your relationship with your wife?"

With a sullen face, Liam replied, "Oh! We loved each other dearly. She was my life! I am so lost without her. We had our highs and lows, but the love was always there."

Ethan nodded. "Can you think of any other prospective suspects?"

Liam rested his head on his hands and said, "As you know, Mr. Carson, Montcherry Luxury is a well-established brand. Business rivalry is, therefore, bound to be present. Other than that, I cannot think of any particular person who would do this to us."

Ethan observed Liam keenly while he spoke, but he maintained a stoic face. He was convinced that Liam loved his wife dearly and could not even dream of murdering her.

Ethan decided to meet the other people relevant to the case.

Liam's house had three live-in maids and two butlers. Ethan met with them one by one and noted their statements. He found nothing of consequence as they all narrated the same thing of not having heard or seen anything during the night of the murder. They looked just as distressed.

Ethan then met with Kelsey Lynskey, Cloe's friend,

who also worked with her at her clothing label. When Ethan asked about Cloe and her attitude in general, Kelsey replied, "Mr. Carson, Cloe was a ruthless businesswoman. Owing to the success and fame the brand had achieved, she considered herself to be a notch above others. Her arrogance was very apparent in all her dealings at the workplace."

Her statement confirmed what Ethan had heard from others as well.

Ethan further inquired, "Tell me about Cloe and Liam's relationship."

Kelsey let out a sigh and shook her head, "At first, all was rosy. But after Liam took to gambling, Cloe started losing her sleep as Liam lost a lot of money. Nonetheless, the love between Liam and Cloe never diminished. Which couple doesn't have differences?"

Ethan nodded and smiled and said, "Thank you for your time, Kelsey. I shall connect with you if I need any other information."

Ethan was known to be a winner, and winning is never easy. He was a perfectionist and a hard worker. By the end of the second day, he had uncovered every aspect of Liam and Cloe's life to understand what he was getting himself into.

Chapter 4

Jury Selection – Behind the Scenes

Jury selection can make the difference between guilt and innocence. Ethan was not one to rely on luck, nor on crossing his fingers and hoping for the best with a randomly assigned jury. He believed in preparation.

A jury list of forty members was compiled by a process of random selection, as per the law. Summons were mailed to these prospective members of the jury. They were even asked to fill a jury qualification questionnaire. Although it only asked for basic information like education, employment, etc., it was an often-neglected tool in high-profile trial strategies.

"Ethan, if I were you, I would for sure try keeping this young lady," advised Bryan, passing the picture of a 23-year-old from a file titled 'Alyssa Carmen'. Ethan was sitting with Bryan, his jury consultant, to make important decisions that could make or break the case.

"Alyssa's uncle had been on trial for murder, though the victim had died in a road accident, in all probability. Her uncle had been at the wrong place at the wrong time. She would most likely rule in favor of Liam and attempt to save him from a wrongful conviction. If the prosecution is unable to find out about this uncle angle, she could be a part of the jury and really help you with your case. She may even fight for you at the time of the verdict," explained Bryan. Ethan nodded in agreement and made a note of her name in his tiny notebook.

"And remember, by no means are you to accept Mr. Forris in the jury. He's a *big* red flag. You must strike him off. His granddaughter was killed by her husband several years ago. He might consider Liam as the husband and Cloe as his granddaughter," informed Bryan.

"Understood," said Ethan as he wrote down 'Samuel Forris' on the other side of the paper in his notebook.

They continued to discuss the other prospective jurors. Bryan explicitly listed out the members that would be favorable and the ones who were to be avoided.

Bryan Watson was Ethan's all-time favorite jury consultant. Ethan hired him for most cases to get as close as possible to a partial jury in his favor. Bryan believed that you win the case long before you hit the courtroom. His goal was to learn as much as possible about the jury before the jury selection even began. Bryan also had a degree in psychology, which made him the perfect person for the job. Not only did he have a team of experienced detectives and psychologists, but he also had a sophisticated high-tech system in place.

They had internal mock trials, where acting jurors had devices attached to their bodies. Bryan tracked the statistics of acting jurors in real time to see how people reacted to a certain piece of evidence or certain behavior of the accused. Jury selection for him was a science, and he and his team had nailed it. The psychology team had mastered the understanding of human behavior and reaction, while his team of detectives were pros at extracting the life history of any person, anywhere in the world.

"Bryan, you are my best-kept secret," Ethan smiled and fondly gave him a pat on the back.

Bryan had always been Ethan's strategic advantage. Though it was common practice to appoint jury consultants, the prosecution had no knowledge about Ethan having hired Bryan, the best in the field, as his jury consultant. Bryan worked discreetly. Ethan's firm willingly paid Bryan's hefty fees as they understood the immense value of his services. It was standard practice for Bryan to do his research and simply send his recommendations by email to his clients. Ethan, however, was no ordinary client. He always spent adequate time with Bryan on the jury selection process, alongside his other trial preparations. Bryan looked up to Ethan for his working style and loved his visits.

It was Sunday evening and Ethan was still at work. The week had flown by quickly with his preparations for Liam's trial.

He drove to his fancy five-bedroom apartment, which was only five minutes away from his office—a luxury that a New Yorker would well appreciate. While driving, Ethan's mind wandered to the time right after his marriage, when they were living in a two-bedroom apartment on the outskirts of New York. He recollected how painful the long drive was back then. Thankfully, he had got a huge promotion soon after, and Sienna's new book had once again become a bestseller at the same time. They had then managed to buy and move into this comfortable upscale apartment close to his workplace.

On reaching home, he was greeted by his two chirpy children at the door. Sienna had missed going to the Hamptons over the weekend, but she knew Ethan was occupied with the big trial. She beamed as the kids set the table and laid out the pizzas. Tonight, was pizza night! They had a good family dinner, post which Ethan tucked his kids into bed. Sienna and Ethan then managed to spend some quality time together, which was rare during trials.

Pregame Huddle

Next morning, Ethan and Michelle were the first ones to reach office for their scheduled early-morning discussion. Though Ethan liked to keep the last day before trial relaxed today was going to be an exception.

Ethan discussed all the aspects of the case with her as they sipped on freshly brewed coffee. As always, Michelle was impressed with Ethan's work. She reminded him once again how important the Montcherry account was for the firm. "Michelle, thank you *sooo* much for the pressure, as if there wasn't enough already," said Ethan sarcastically as he went back to his office.

He had meetings scheduled throughout the day. The first half of the day was with Bryan, and the second half was with Liam. Food was ordered as his team had a working lunch in between the two meetings. Ethan eventually dismissed the last meeting at 6 p.m. and went back to his office. He reread through every detail of the case meticulously till he felt satisfied with his preparation.

The next day was jury selection. If Ethan was to be productive, he needed to get a good night's sleep. Eventually, he put down the files, shut his laptop, and walked out of his office while flashing his charming smile. He drove back home in his Persian blue BMW and went over the case one last time at home before he inevitably fell asleep.

Ethan felt confident; he was ready to protect his client, Liam Montcherry.

Chapter 5
Voir Dire

It was the day of voir dire, the jury selection.

A few reporters and onlookers had gathered outside the court. Though it was a high-profile case, the crowd was relatively thin as it was only the jury selection day, with less scope of courtroom drama. Ethan shrugged at the thought of how this place would transform during the coming trial days.

The courtroom, however, was abuzz. The prosecutor and his associate sat on one side of the courtroom, while Ethan and his associate, Martin sat on the other side. The row behind Ethan and his associate had two attorneys from Bennett International. Ethan liked to have some attorneys attend all proceedings of his high-profile cases so that he could have backup in case of an emergency. They were, however, dressed discretely as per Ethan's instructions so as to not intimidate the jury. Was Ethan meticulous, or what?

The randomly selected panel of the forty potential jurors of the jury pool sat in the public sitting area of the courtroom. Some members were hoping to get the privilege of being on the jury and help deliver justice, while others were hoping to not be stuck with jury duty all week.

"I always wonder why it's called jury selection when it is actually more of a jury rejection. We cannot select a single jury of choice; rather, we can only eliminate the ones we don't find suitable," commented Martin.

Ethan nodded at Martin and said, "Well, you are right, but this day is critical to any case. It is the only day attorneys can talk one-on-one with the jury."

Martin was impressed by Ethan's perspective.

While everyone remained seated and waited for the judge to arrive, Ethan walked over to the prosecutor's side and said, "Hello." He shook the prosecutor's hand and continued, "Ethan Carson."

The prosecutor nodded his head and said, "Jacob Harris. Pleasure to meet you—I have heard great things about you."

Ethan was not particularly excited about Jacob being the prosecutor. He had never had the opportunity to face him in any earlier trial, though he had studied some of Jacob's cases and had found him to be sharp and shrewd.

He remembered well the rumor that had spread several years ago that Jacob liked to work in the gray. Jacob had crossed certain lines and wasn't proud of it. Many said that over the years, he had skirted the law more than any other prosecutor. It's usually the defense attorneys who worked in that fashion. It made a whole lot of sense, considering he wanted to be a defense lawyer at first but changed his mind when he got a good job as a prosecutor.

Ethan smirked and said, "Well, if you have heard so much about me, you already know that you are going to lose."

Jacob chuckled briefly in disbelief. "Mr. Carson, I have heard about you, hence I know all your tactics. However, you don't know much about me, and that gives me the advantage in this situation." He shook his head before continuing. "Anyways, I'm not the one to pick a fight." He then pointed towards the young man seated next to him and said, "This is my associate, Zach Peterson. He's been working with me for the past three years."

Ethan looked at Jacob's associate, then back at Jacob, and said, "Well, Zach. 'Tis a pleasure to meet ya. This is my associate, Martin Diaz. However, he has not been working for me for years or even months; rather, only a few weeks. You see, I don't have my associates solve cases for me; I solve them myself. I only trust my own work. You will soon find out that my tactics, as you call them, are absolutely unique for every case."

Before Jacob could respond, Ethan nodded briefly at him and his associate and walked back over to his side of the court. Martin hurriedly followed Ethan and took his seat beside him.

This was the first case assigned to Martin, and he already felt like he was on a roller coaster ride, thanks to Ethan's style of working.

"All rise. This court is now in session. The Honorable Judge Nicholas Trevino presiding," announced the bailiff, Mikael Melroy.

Everyone stood up to show respect for the judge, the court, and the law.

Judge Nicholas was in his early 60s and was soon to be retiring. Over the years, he had gained the reputation of being a kind-hearted and fair judge. He was just, and didn't let his personal bias interfere with his duty in court.

Before he was appointed as judge, he was a defense lawyer, and a damn good one, too—some might even say the best. He was the Ethan Carson of two decades ago, except that he never worked in the gray. Even then, Judge Nicholas always followed the law to the crisp, though he was very selective of the cases he took. All he cared about then was winning, but when he was appointed as judge, he knew he had to be fair. He always took into consideration the story from both sides and then analyzed the situation before coming to a decision.

In the courtroom, the potential jurors were then asked to take an oath with raised right hands; they promised to answer all questions truthfully.

"If there are any members present here in the jury pool who have a reason as to why they will not be able to serve on the case, please speak now." Judge Nicholas began the voir dire.

No one spoke.

"That's good. We have a group of responsible citizens in court today," said the judge with a slight smile.

Some members looked fidgety as they wanted to be spared from jury duty but could not come up with any excuse.

Judge looked at the bailiff and said, "Mr. Melroy, please note that no summoned members present here have any reason to be exempted from jury duty."

Jury selection began with the court's clerk calling twelve people from the pool of forty on the jury list and asking them to take their place in the jury box. This was to be a petit jury, where six to twelve jurors are selected; in this case, there were going to be twelve. One by one, their names were called out and they were each assigned a juror number, starting with number 1. The jury box had two rows with six seats each. The named potential jurors took their seats, starting from the corner seat in the back row of the jury box.

Ethan held his head as he heard the name of Mrs. Kristan Woods being called out as part of the twelve jurors. Bryan had warned him about her during their discussions. Mrs. Woods' niece had been murdered a decade back by a family member, which had left her shattered. Ethan was to reject her, since she could be biased in a murder trial. Mrs. Woods was jury number 9, and Ethan made a note to strike her off the final jury.

Ethan was delighted by jury number 11, Alyssa Carmen. But at the back of his mind, he had a hunch that Jacob would also have done some homework on the jury pool, and Alyssa's uncle being on trial could have come up. He kept his fingers crossed and hoped for her selection by the prosecution.

Judge Nicholas then addressed the potential jurors. "Ladies and gentlemen of the jury, this is a criminal case. By the end of the day, you will know if you are going to be serving as a juror on this case. I will brief you about the case now. The defendant, Liam Montcherry, is being charged with the murder of his wife, Cloe Montcherry, in the first degree. At the end of the trial, you must impartially decide whether or not Liam Montcherry is guilty beyond reasonable doubt. The basis of your verdict should only be deduced from what is going to be discussed in the court during the upcoming trial."

Since this was a high-profile case, the judge further instructed the jury, "You must refrain from hearing or reading about the case or the defendant on social media or TV, as it could cloud your judgment. Furthermore, you are not allowed to speak about the defendant or the case with anyone." He went on to emphasize, "If anyone approaches you with regard to the case, you are to immediately inform the bailiff or me."

"Jury number 8, Mr. Taylor Davis, you seem to be injured," enquired the judge, as he noticed the young man had his left arm in a plaster.

"Yes, Your Honor. I had a terrible fall and have a fractured hand," replied Mr. Davis, as he stood up.

"I see. Will you be able to carry out your jury duty diligently despite the injury?" asked the judge.

Mr. Davis was quick to reassure the judge as he replied, "Yes, Your Honor. This will not interfere with my obligations towards the country."

Judge Nicholas nodded with respect for the man

and asked him to take his seat. He then pointed towards the attorneys and said, "Mr. Jacob Harris here is the prosecutor, which means that he will be arguing from the state's side, while Mr. Ethan Carson here is the defense lawyer and will be arguing from the defendant's side."

The judge then introduced Liam Montcherry, the defendant, to the prospective jury.

The names of the witnesses who were going to be summoned during the progression of the trial were announced for the jury members' knowledge.

The members on the stand made note of the sudden flood of information being directed their way.

After Judge Nicholas was done with the introductions, it was the attorneys' turn to ask questions to the prospective jury on the stand, looking for bias to eliminate.

Prosecutor Jacob began by greeting the twelve selected members sitting in the stand. "Good morning, ladies and gentlemen. My name is Jacob Harris. Simply put, my job is to take all the evidence from the police and present them in court."

The prospective jury listened to him intently.

Jacob then asked the potential jurors a series of questions to find out if there was any reason, they might have to be biased. He faced the jurors and inquired if they had ever been convicted for a crime, been the victim of a crime, been known to any of the attorneys or witnesses, been a juror before, or if had any reason whatsoever to be partial.

The jurors answered the questions to Jacob's

satisfaction, after which, he returned to his seat and made some notes in his writing pad.

Ethan heaved a sigh of relief as Jacob had no direct question for Alyssa Carmen, jury number 11. He had been hoping that Jacob was unaware of Alyssa's background and would retain her. However, he couldn't be completely sure of this till Jacob announced the names of the jurors he wanted to strike off.

It was then the defense attorney, Ethan's, turn for questioning. He was well-prepared. He had already received his list of questions from Bryan, his jury consultant. Bryan had the lives of each of the forty members of the jury pool documented. He had given Ethan seven names with red flags that he was to reject. Bryan had prepared specific questions for each of these members that Ethan was to ask. Luckily, only Mrs. Woods had been selected from his red flag list so far.

Ethan got up and faced the jurors with a well-practiced subtle smile. He started by asking generic questions to the jury with keen interest, so as to not make it obvious that he had a jury consultant with an army of detectives and psychologists at his disposal. All potential jurors answered the questions to his satisfaction.

Ethan then asked his only specific question that was pre-written against Mrs. Woods' name.

"Has anyone in your circle of friends or extended family been murdered?" asked Ethan, glancing at all the jurors.

Mrs. Woods reluctantly raised her hand with great despair and softly said, "Yes, my niece." Her sad tone of voice revealed that time had not healed her wound of losing her little niece.

At moments like these, Ethan felt proud of Bryan. Though he felt elated, he maintained a solemn face and uttered with utmost respect, "I am sorry to hear about your loss. I have no more questions." He then walked back to his seat and sat down.

"Counsel approach," stated Judge Nicholas.

Both attorneys walked up to him. In a low voice, Judge Nicholas called out names of each of the twelve potential jurors one by one. The attorneys confirmed if they were 'good for the state/defense' to be jurors or 'striked' and were to go home.

There were three strikes in all. Jacob struck-off jury number 5 and 7, while Ethan struck off jury number 9.

Jacob's face fell as the defense struck off his favorite, jury number 9. His hopes of retaining this jury had anyway been shattered when Mrs. Woods admitted in court that her niece had been murdered. As a competent attorney, Jacob knew that Ethan would strike her off after having this knowledge.

Ethan, on the other hand, was elated that Alyssa remained as a juror; he could already visualize her rooting for his client.

The judge then announced the names of jury number 5, 7, and 9. He informed them that they could go home and continued, "You must understand that not getting selected for jury duty in no way means that you are not fit to be on the jury. If any of you are having such thoughts, you must understand this. Not getting selected only means that the attorneys here feel that you will not be able to come to an impartial judgment given your past and the nature of this particular case. I thank you for your time and service. You may leave."

Three new jurors were called on the stand from the remaining jury pool as jury number 5, 7 and 9 left the stand. The prosecution and defense repeated the cycle of asking the three new potential jurors their questions. The judge again called counsel to approach, and this time, both attorneys were satisfied with all the jurors.

The jury was selected.

The judge addressed the final jury. "You have been selected to be the jury for this trial. You are to be on time on all days of the trial and assist in delivering justice in this case. In a moment, I am going to ask you to go into the jury room and select a foreperson from amongst you. This person will act as your spokesperson throughout the trial. Any communication by the jury will need to be made only through this person. You may now proceed. Elect your foreperson by vote, and return to the courtroom."

The jury was then escorted to the jury room that was adjoining the courtroom. After some deliberation, the jury came back with a certain Mrs. Clarisse Gardner, an old lady in her sixties, as their foreperson.

Judge Nicholas accepted the foreperson and gave her sitting instructions. "Mrs. Gardner, since all jury communication will happen through you, you will be seated in the seat closest to me as well as the microphone. Anything that is said will thereby be easily recorded."

Mrs. Gardner nodded in agreement and took the corner seat in the front row of the jury box. Judge Nicholas dismissed the court for the day. The trial was to begin the next day.

Interestingly, the jury for this murder trial consisted of eight men and four women. There were two old women in their sixties, while the other two were well below the age of thirty. The men, however, were all below the age of forty-five. Ethan was content that there were no red flags as per Bryan in the selected jury.

Ethan had already won this case, if Bryan was to be believed.

Chapter 6

The Trial

Day 1, Wednesday, the Action Begins

On the first day of trial, all witnesses, the defendant, the lawyers, the jury, and other people involved in the case, showed up in court right on time. Looking at the large crowd gathered outside today, one could easily tell that it was a high-profile case. A flurry of journalists gathered outside the court in anticipation of some controversial content for their publications.

As Liam and Ethan exited their cars, a huge crowd surrounded them. Reporters bombarded them with questions. They ignored the crowd and managed to enter the court.

Halfway through the courtroom, Liam's mother ran up to Liam and hugged him. She prayed for her son's acquittal. Liam felt overwhelmed as he noticed his father, brother, cousin, and half-sister sitting in the public sitting area in his support.

The public sitting area also had some distraught faces. Sitting there, as if in a state of shock were Cloe Montcherry's mother Mrs. Olson who had come along with her sister.

Liam continued walking and sat with Ethan and his associate Martin in the first row. Martin looked back to greet the two attorneys from his firm, sitting in the row behind them.

Jacob Harris was already in place on the other side of the courtroom, browsing through some files.

There was an air of nervous excitement in the courtroom.

"All rise," announced the bailiff as he informed the court of the judge's arrival.

Judge Nicholas entered and asked everyone to be seated. Court was now in session.

The judge looked at the bailiff and instructed him, "Mr. Melroy, please bring in the jury."

The bailiff escorted the jury members inside the court. All twelve members of the jury walked in, looking fresh and ready for the trial.

"Mr. Melroy, please swear in the jury," the judge further instructed. The bailiff faced the jurors and said, "Please raise your right hand. Do you solemnly swear or affirm that you will listen to this case and render a true verdict for the defendant, Mr. Liam Montcherry?"

"I do." The members of the jury answered with their right hand raised.

The bailiff then stated, "You may be seated." The members of the jury took their seats.

The judge addressed the jury. "Ladies and gentlemen of the jury, this is the trial of a criminal case. The defendant, Mr. Liam Montcherry, is charged with murder in the first degree. It is my duty as the judge to instruct you on the law in this case. The law states that in every criminal case, the defendant is presumed to be innocent *unless* proven guilty beyond a reasonable doubt by the prosecutor. The law does not require the defendant to prove his innocence or to produce any evidence. At the end of the trial, you must find the defendant not guilty unless the prosecution has proved to you beyond a reasonable doubt that the defendant has committed the offense with which he is charged."

The court was informed about the delay in the autopsy report and that it would be made available by Monday. The information was noted.

Judge Nicholas took a brief pause and then addressed the prosecution and defense attorneys. "We shall now begin. Are both parties ready to make their opening statements?"

The attorneys responded, "Yes, Your Honor."

"You may proceed," said the judge.

As per the law, the prosecutor stood and presented his opening statement first. "Your Honor, counsel, ladies, and gentlemen of the jury, my name is Jacob Harris, and I am representing the prosecution. The prosecution pleads Liam Montcherry to be guilty of the murder of his wife. As the trial progresses, you will see the way a young lady was murdered in cold blood by her husband on the night of their first wedding anniversary. At the end of the trial, I am sure that you will find the defendant, Liam Montcherry, guilty of murder." Jacob spoke with conviction. Jacob Harris was a prominent lawyer and was known for coming up with firm evidence.

It was now Ethan's turn to give his opening statement. "Your Honor, counsel, ladies, and gentlemen of the jury, my name is Ethan Carson, and I am representing the defendant. My statement is, however, way simpler than Mr. Harris' over there. I shall provide concrete proof that my client was not involved in this murder in any way. I would also like to state that Mr. Montcherry did not have *any* motive to kill his wife. In fact, he was the person who called the police as soon as he discovered her body in the first place. I am certain that you will return a verdict of *not guilty* once you have learnt about all the evidence." Ethan spoke confidently.

As Ethan turned around to sit, his eyes met Jacob's. That brief yet powerful gaze was enough to indicate that a brutal battle of mind and words had only just begun.

Their gaze was interrupted by the judge's announcement. "The prosecutor may now call its first witness."

Jacob Harris said, "Yes, Your Honor. I call to the stand Mrs. Olson."

The judge instructed the bailiff to call her in and proceed with the swearing in.

Mr. Melroy escorted Mrs. Olson to the witness stand and said to her, "Please raise your right hand. Do you swear to tell the truth, the whole truth, and nothing but the truth?"

"I do," she said with a raised hand and sat down.

Mr. Harris faced the judge and introduced his first witness. "Your Honor, this is Mrs. Olson, Cloe Montcherry's mother."

He then turned towards Mrs. Olson and continued, "Mrs. Olson, I am sorry for your loss. I cannot begin to imagine the pain it must have caused to you, losing your daughter only a year into her marriage. I have a few questions I need to ask you. Did you ever hear anything of concern from the deceased before the murder?"

"Objection, Your Honor. Vague," said Ethan in a holier-than-thou tone of voice.

"Sustained," said the judge.

"Let me be more specific," continued Mr. Harris. "Mrs. Olson, did you speak to your daughter on the day of the incident?"

"Yes, I did. I had called to wish her in the morning, as it was her wedding anniversary," replied Mrs. Olson.

"Did you speak to her after that?" asked Mr. Harris.

"No, no… I did not. Cloe called me several times late that night, though unfortunately we could not speak. I was asleep then. She normally never called at such late hours. I only saw the missed calls early in the morning, but by that time, it was too late. People are saying, the murder happened very late at night. How I wish I was up when she called. I could have saved her," sobbed Mrs. Olson.

Mr. Harris gave her a minute as she calmed herself down. He then continued, "Mrs. Olson, how did Cloe sound on the phone that morning? Did she say anything about Liam?"

"Though Cloe was trying to sound happy about their celebration plans for the day, I could sense that she was upset. She had also mentioned to me that morning that she had had a fight with Liam the previous day," Mrs. Olson replied.

Mr. Harris looked at the jury members and repeated with emphasis, *"Cloe and Liam had a fight the day before her murder, and Cloe was upset about it."*

Several members of the jury nodded, as if making a mental note of the information.

Mrs. Olson continued, "This was not the first time my Cloe had told me about their fights. I assumed them to be general husband-wife arguments and chose not to interfere. I had no idea it would lead to the death of my dear, sweet baby," she sniffed. She looked like she was about to cry, but somehow she managed to hold back her tears.

"I agree, Mrs. Olson. The couple having had continued arguments and fights, especially on the day prior to the murder, is too much of a coincidence to ignore," said Mr. Harris.

"Your Honor, I would now like to bring the phone records and phone dial history records of the victim to the court's attention," said Mr. Harris as he passed the file to the clerk. The clerk handed it over to the judge after making a note of it.

Mr. Harris then continued, "The unanswered calls that Mrs. Olson received at an odd hour on the night of the murder, indicate that the deceased was trying to reach for help. Cloe even tried calling 911 after her failed attempts at reaching her mother, as you can see in the dial history of Cloe's cell phone. Unfortunately, the call was disconnected from her end even before it could connect to 911. The phone was later found broken and shattered to pieces, clearly indicating that the killer would have destroyed the phone as she tried to call the police. I have no further questions, Your Honor."

The judge checked the file and confirmed that the victim had made attempts to call her mother and the police on the night of her murder.

Judge Nicholas then looked at Ethan and said, "The defense may now cross-examine the witness."

Ethan walked up to Mrs. Olson, looked at Mr. Harris, and then gazed back at her and said, "Mrs. Olson, how close were you with your daughter? Did she always share her problems with you?"

"She was my only child; we were very close. She always shared everything about her life with me," answered Mrs. Olson.

"When was the last time you spoke to your daughter prior to her anniversary?" continued Ethan.

"We spoke almost every day. For the last one month, she had been telling me about her fights with Liam over calls," she replied with a deep frown.

"Mrs. Olson, according to your phone records, Cloe hadn't spoken to you over the phone for over a month prior to her anniversary. Then how can you say that she told you over calls about continued fights she had with her husband?" demanded Ethan.

There was a gasp from the spectators which was followed by complete silence in the court. Jacob hurriedly fumbled through the copy of Mrs. Olson's phone records, clearly caught off guard.

Hesitantly, the woman said, "We might have spoken through another phone. She may have been at a friend's house and used their phone. I am not sure why the records don't show it, but we spoke, and she told me about the fights with Liam."

Ethan raised his brows in disbelief. These days, who calls someone from a friend's landline and not their mobile phone, he wondered? Out loud, he said, "Well, Mrs. Olson, that does not really prove anything as there are no records to back what you are saying. Moving on, were you and Liam close to one another?"

She replied, "Yes. Pretty much, I would say. We invited him to all family functions and vacations. He also loved visiting us over the weekends."

Ethan responded thoughtfully, "Well then, why are there no call records between you two as well? I mean, surely you would inform each other over calls before showing up for weekends. Or is it that you did not approve of Mr. Montcherry? Is that the reason you are making up the story of Cloe calling you to discuss their fights?"

"Objection, Your Honor, leading," interrupted Mr. Harris.

"Sustained," said the judge.

"Withdrawn," nodded Ethan.

Ethan reframed his question. "Mrs. Olson, did you approve of Mr. Montcherry?"

"Yes, I did. My daughter loved him and so did my family and I. Like I said earlier, we were close to one another," she replied.

"Did you recently directly talk to Mr. Montcherry on the phone or otherwise?" asked Ethan.

"Yes, we did speak on the phone," she replied.

"Then, Mrs. Olson, can you please explain to the court why there are no call records?" he asked, looking up in frustration.

Mrs. Olson just looked down and sobbed, unable to come up with an answer.

After a while, the judge reminded her, "Mrs. Olson, you are obligated to answer the question."

The old lady composed herself, coughed a little and said, "Well, maybe because we usually spoke through Cloe's phone or her home landline number."

"Mrs. Olson, there are no call records on either of your cell phones or landline phones to back your story. Are you making this up?" demanded Ethan.

"Objection, argumentative," said Mr. Harris.

"Sustained," said the judge.

"Withdrawn," said Ethan, annoyed as hell.

Just then, Ethan noticed Liam trying to bring his attention to a piece of paper in his hand, rather slyly.

Ethan moved to his table on the pretext of drinking some water from his glass. He was shocked as he read the note that Liam had been trying to show him. It read 'Dementia' in big, bold letters. Ethan's mind was racing as he tried to make sense of it. He did not want to argue in court with half-baked information. He had to think of something quickly; time was not on his side right now.

He addressed the judge and said empathetically, "Your Honor, I would like a fifteen-minute recess to help Mrs. Olson relax a bit. I have more questions for her."

Judge Nicholas looked at Jacob, who nodded in agreement. "That is thoughtful of you, Mr. Carson. We shall all meet in 30 minutes. All of us could do with a break. Court is in recess," announced the judge as he left for his chambers.

Ethan dropped in his seat, mentally exhausted at not being in control of his case. As he took a sneak peek at the prosecution, he was glad to see Jacob and his team leaving the courtroom. Ethan could now talk peacefully and in private. Liam and Martin started talking simultaneously, and Ethan understood none of it.

"Calm down, both of you. Liam, you go first. Do you miss being in school? What is this about passing chits? It's a courtroom, for God's sake! Hurry up now, we don't have much time," said an exasperated Ethan.

"Well, my mother-in-law has been on medication for dementia for almost two years. Over time, her condition has only deteriorated. She has trouble remembering things and even had hallucinatory episodes. This must be the reason she is insisting on phone calls that never happened," informed Liam.

"And you didn't find it important to bring it to me earlier?" demanded Ethan.

"Absolutely not, Ethan. I did not know she would start accusing me in court of continuously fighting with Cloe," explained Liam.

"We have to find a way to prove Mrs. Olson's medical condition in court," Ethan thought aloud.

"That's simple. Liam could call her neurologist and get her records. He could say he's concerned about her health and wants to understand her medical history," suggested Martin.

"Think straight, Martin. No doctor would divulge a patient's condition to a suspect who is being tried in court. The case is all over the news. We will have to think of another way. Liam, how sure are you about Mrs. Olson's dementia?" asked Ethan, his mind racing.

"100 percent, Ethan, I have even accompanied her to the doctor a few times with Cloe," confirmed Liam.

"All right, at this point in time, we have no other option but to bank on your understanding of Mrs. Olson's medical condition. Martin, you check up on Mrs. Olson's doctor's credentials right away and confirm if he is a subject matter expert to be able to testify in court about Mrs. Olson's medical condition," instructed Ethan.

Liam shared the doctor's details with Martin. He was relieved he had the phone number handy. Cloe had saved it on both their phones for emergency situations.

Ethan thought over it and then inquired, "I would like to have a clear picture about your relationship with Cloe. Why did Mrs. Olson insist that Cloe and you had a fight the day before your anniversary? You told me things were great between the two of you." Ethan waited for Liam's answer, looking intently at him and, resting his elbows on the desk while clasping his hands beneath his chin.

Liam sighed. "Well, it's not that Cloe and I never fought, but we definitely did not have a fight the day before our anniversary. As I informed you during our initial meetings, I had lost a large sum of money gambling around four months back. Cloe was very upset about it. Though I had decided never to gamble again, our fights were mostly centered around it. But this was months back. Cloe may have discussed these fights with her mother back then." He then shrugged and continued, "I don't know why Mrs. Olson is insisting about the fight a day before our anniversary. Though I feel she wouldn't lie about her daughter's calls, she may have got the timing all mixed up in her head. She has just lost her daughter and is on heavy medication."

Just then, Martin ran back to them and confirmed that Mrs. Olson's doctor was eligible to testify on dementia. Ethan spent some time processing it all and strategized his next move.

The 30-minute break ended, and the court got back into session. Mrs. Olson was brought back in the witness stand. She looked visibly calm and better composed now.

Ethan stood up and began with confidence, "Before we begin, Your Honor, it has come to our attention that

Mrs. Olson is going through medical treatment and is on medication to help with her mental condition. She suffers from dementia, hence whatever she has said should be inadmissible in court."

"Objection, Your Honor. Hearsay," shouted Jacob. Mrs. Olson was his prime witness, and he was not going to let her testimony be made inadmissible so easily.

"Sustained. Mr. Carson, do you have any means to verify this?" asked Judge Nicolas.

"Withdrawn for now, Your Honor. I will soon verify this. I would like to continue examining Mrs. Olson," he said.

Judge Nicholas nodded and replied, "Please go ahead."

Ethan stood facing Mrs. Olson and inquired, "Mrs. Olson, is it true that you are suffering from dementia?"

"Yes, I am, but I know for sure that Cloe was unhappy and had frequent arguments with Liam," she declared rather defensively.

Ethan then turned towards the judge and moved his gaze over all the jury members slowly, his voice oozing with conviction as he said, "Your Honor, dementia is a term for the impaired ability to remember, think, or make decisions, among other things."

"Mrs. Olson, are you seeing any doctor for this, and are you on any kind of medication?" enquired Ethan.

"Oh yes, I've been on medication for over two years now, and I am more than fit to testify. You can ask my doctor," said Mrs. Olson, falling into Ethan's trap.

Ethan instantly said, "Thank you for your consent, Mrs. Olson. Your Honor, I would request Mrs. Olson's neurologist to be summoned to court to testify on her dementia stage and medical condition."

Jacob couldn't believe how the case suddenly took a completely different direction. He fumed, "Objection, Your Honor. Badgering!"

The judge took into consideration the consent given by Mrs. Olson herself and uttered, "Overruled."

To this, Mrs. Olson responded, "Yes, that would be best. My doctor would confirm that I am completely sane and fit to testify. No one can stop me from punishing my darling daughter's killer."

The judge ordered that the neurologist be subpoenaed to appear and testify in the next hearing.

"No further questions, Your Honor," concluded Ethan as he returned to his seat, completely satisfied with the proceedings.

Mr. Harris looked furious as he saw his prime witness crumble his case. He had clearly underestimated the importance of Mrs. Olson's testimony. He had used her only as a grieving mother card and did not delve much into her background, a mistake that was turning out to be expensive.

It was time for the second witness to be called upon and fresh evidence to be provided. Mr. Harris requested to call for Mathew Davis as his next witness. The bailiff escorted Mathew to the witness stand, introductions were made, and the oath was taken.

Jacob began by asking, "Mr. Davis, where were you between 11 p.m. and 6 a.m. on the night of the murder?"

Mathew replied, "I was at home, having a movie night with friends."

"Who all were present with you?" asked Jacob.

"Liam was there," replied Mathew. Then after a thoughtful pause, he added, "My friend Christopher, his girlfriend Lola, and my sister Jacky were also there."

Mr. Harris walked closer to the stand and said, "Mr. Davis, did your friend, Liam ever leave the house on that night between 11 p.m. and 6 a.m.? It could be for any reason at all. Was he gone for a short period of time, even as less as ten minutes?"

Mathew thought for a while and then said, "I think he was the one who got pizza from the nearby 24-hour gas station."

"Are you sure it was Liam who went to get the pizza?" asked Mr. Harris.

"Yes, I am very sure it was Liam," nodded Mathew.

"How long was he gone for precisely?" asked Mr. Harris.

"Well, I would say 40 to 45 minutes," replied Mathew.

"Aha! Your Honor, keeping in mind, that the traffic is rather low so late at night, Mr. Montcherry could have easily gone back home, killed his wife, and got pizza from the gas station, all within 45 minutes," stated Mr. Harris with satisfaction. "I have no further questions," concluded Mr. Harris.

"Do you wish to cross-examine, Mr. Carson?" the judge asked Ethan.

Ethan stood up and nodded saying, "Yes, Your Honor, I do."

He moved to the front of the witness stand and started his questioning. "Mr. Davis, was it the first time that you were having a late-night party at your house with Liam?"

"No, we all meet very often," answered Mathew.

"Who usually goes to get the last-minute food, drinks, etc.? Do you all take turns for it?" enquired Ethan.

"Well, no, it is mostly Liam who goes to pick up pizza, drinks, etc. He has a car and also knows the area well since he lives close by," informed Mathew.

"You mean to say it was nothing out of the ordinary that Liam volunteered to get the pizza that night?" Asked Ethan, wanting to confirm the point to convince the jury.

"Not at all. It was always him," confirmed Mathew.

"Mr. Davis, on Mr. Montcherry's return with the pizza, did you notice anything suspicious about him, like maybe torn clothes, scratch marks, or any blood on him?" enquired Ethan.

"No, sir. I noticed nothing like that when he came back with the pizza," Mathew replied, shaking his head.

"Mr. Davis, I want you to visualize the moment when Mr. Montcherry returned that night. Now try to recall if you could sense any signs of nervousness or guilt from him," inquired Ethan.

Mathew paused to recall, while the jury waited for his answer in anticipation.

"No, Liam seemed in a very jovial mood and was excited to eat the pizza on his return. He was his usual self," elaborated Mathew.

Liam's family sitting in the public sitting area breathed a sigh of relief.

Ethan looked at the judge with a satisfied expression and said, "Your Honor, we can safely come to the most obvious conclusion. My client, Liam has an alibi that proves him being with his friends that night. Just because he went to get pizza like he always does, doesn't prove that he murdered his wife on the way. Since he was with his friends all night, there was no way that he could be the killer." Ethan paused for the alibi to sink into the jury's mind and then continued, "I have no further questions."

Mathew was dismissed as the questioning ended. He gulped down a 500 ml bottle of water on taking his seat in the public sitting area, shaken at being dragged into a murder trial.

Though Ethan was relieved he could cover up Liam's alibi for now, he knew the 20-minute time lag in the alibi was going to hit him hard in the future.

The judge announced, "The court is adjourned for the day. The court shall resume on Friday as tomorrow is a federal holiday."

The older members of the jury looked visibly happy with the holiday announcement. It had been a long day, and they seemed tired.

While everyone was relaxed after the holiday announcement, Ethan's mind raced to plan a productive extra day. Ethan did not have the concept of mid-trial holidays. Once a trial started, his holiday only began when he won the case.

Chapter 7

The Trial

Thursday, Mid-Trial Holiday

The next day, Ethan decided to have a talk with Liam and asked him to come to his office.

To Ethan's liking, Liam reached right on time. While the two were in the midst of their discussion, Timothy dropped by for an early lunch with Ethan.

Ethan introduced him to Liam. "This is my best friend, Dr. Timothy Ann, who is also my advisor on matters of medical nature related to my cases. He sometimes watches my trials from the public seating area for his love for the law and me," joked Ethan.

Liam was in no mood for jokes or socializing. He nodded slightly at Timothy and focused back on Ethan.

Ethan sensed his mood and got back to their discussion related to the trial. Timothy made himself comfortable on his favorite couch in Ethan's large office. He picked up Sienna's latest book from Ethan's bookshelf and began reading it as he waited for his lunch out with Ethan.

"Liam, you know you go on the stand tomorrow. I hope you are prepared to answer all the questions that may be asked by the prosecution in court," inquired Ethan.

"Yes, you have already briefed me well on it before the trial began. I am ready," replied Liam.

"That's good to hear. Liam, if there is anything you haven't shared with me, now is the time. You know that I can only protect you if you are honest and transparent with me," inquired Ethan.

Liam hesitated and then replied, "Well, there might have been something I missed telling you. I have a close friend by the name of Elijah Taylor. He is a financial consultant and has been my constant advisor on financial matters. After I got married, he had advised me to take up an insurance policy. I had listened to him and had taken out life insurance policies for both Cloe and myself in the first month of our marriage."

Ethan felt dizzy as he took in this new information. He was less upset with Liam for sharing this information so late, and more upset with his own self for not having checked on this point earlier. Ethan had assumed that Liam was too young and irresponsible to have thought about insurance. For the first time in his career, he had a moment of self-doubt. 'Am I losing my edge?' he thought to himself.

He calmed himself and said, "Liam, are you aware that an insurance policy gives the beneficiary an obvious motive to kill?!" Thinking further, he asked, "Is anyone else aware of this policy?"

"Yes, my mother-in-law is aware of it. In fact, Mrs. Olson was against it as she believed that taking life insurance policy at a young age would bring bad luck. Cloe had ultimately managed to convince her before we went ahead with it," answered Liam.

"I am surprised neither your mother-in-law nor the prosecution has brought it up in court yet. Anyway, her whole testimony would be inadmissible once the neurologist affirms her mental disorder in court tomorrow. But still, what if she had bought it up? I would have been caught off guard," said Ethan in disbelief. He hated it when his clients kept vital information from him.

"I would like to believe that she hasn't mentioned it as she trusts me enough and does not want me to go to prison. Like you rightly said, this would count as a clear motive for murder," mumbled Liam.

"Or maybe it's due to dementia and she has no memory of it now," interrupted Ethan. "It was clever of you to write dementia on the piece of paper yesterday during trial. It saved our case in more ways than one, as is apparent now. A grieving mother never works well for the murder suspect," Ethan shrugged.

He then added, "Liam, you should have disclosed the insurance policy prior to the hearing. I hope that you are not keeping any more secrets from me. If the prosecution knows about the insurance policy, they will definitely bring it up while you are on the stand tomorrow. They would also leave no stone unturned to prove that this insurance money was your motive to murder your wife."

Liam sat tight-lipped as he realized the enormity of it all.

Ethan then moved on to the more important question. "How much is this policy worth?" he enquired.

"It is for 50 million dollars," Liam disclosed.

"50 million dollars?!" exclaimed Ethan. He could see the prosecution butchering Liam in court the next day. It was too large a sum.

"Liam, we must disclose the policy to court ourselves. Sooner or later, the prosecution will bring it up. Tomorrow, when you go on the stand, it will look bad if the prosecution brings this up and not you yourself. Trust me and my experience on this," insisted Ethan.

"No way am I going to take that chance! I am paying you to defend me, and you will do as I say or you will be fired like my last attorney," demanded Liam.

Ethan's managing partner had reminded him over and over how much the firm needed his account, and that Liam needed to be kept happy during the trial. Ethan was now finding it difficult to keep him happy and out of prison at the same time.

"Well then, though it's highly unlikely, let's hope no one finds out about the insurance policy if you have to be kept out of prison. I am legally bound to disclose this myself to court upon discovery, so let's assume we never had this conversation," said a frustrated Ethan. He did not want to commit to perjury, but Liam was adamant about not disclosing the policy, and he felt he had no choice.

"We never had this conversation," repeated Liam and nodded in agreement. He was scared and had not wanted to disclose the insurance policy as he knew it would be considered a motive. Better sense had prevailed today, and he had decided to trust his lawyer and share it with him.

Ethan's mind wandered to Jacob Harris. "Even if the prosecution brings it up, which I'm sure they will, I'll brief you well, and we will be prepared with a damn good argument," continued Ethan with concern. Ethan spent some time prepping Liam for any prospective questions that might come his way regarding the insurance money. Liam, however, seemed convinced that the prosecution would not know about it and therefore, kept calling the exercise a waste of time, to Ethan's frustration.

Liam convinced Ethan that he had shared everything else transparently with him and he was ready for his testimony.

On that note, they ended their meeting. Liam left for his home while Ethan and Timothy took off for their lunch. Timothy complimented Sienna's book and took it with him with a promise to return it on completion.

Ethan was in no mood for lunch and wanted to start working on the unexpected issues that had cropped up. Timothy, his dear friend, did not budge and dragged him to their favorite café, À La Cheese, as planned. Timothy wanted to help him relax. Eventually, Ethan did relax and to his surprise, even enjoyed the lunch with Timothy. Timothy spoke about some hilarious events at his hospital with a new patient. Ethan thought about how good it was to get his mind off the case for a while and enjoy the company of his friend. He smiled as he dug into his favorite mud pie for dessert.

Ethan went straight to his office post lunch. He had to work on his defense for the critical information he had received from Liam about the large sum of insurance money. As he was about to wrap up for the day, he got an email from Martin, his associate. It had information regarding all that he was required to know about Mrs. Olson's neurologist, for his testimony the next morning. Ethan was relieved to read it.

He gathered his thoughts and prepared himself for the next day's trial.

Chapter 8

The Trial
Day 2, Friday,
The Defendant on the Stand

All involved parties returned to court on Friday, ready for the second day of trial.

Judge Nicholas entered the court, sat on his chair, and said, "Be seated. We shall continue."

The jury entered and took their seats after taking their oath.

Mrs. Olson's neurologist, Dr. Kol Woods was called to the witness stand. Dr. Woods looked quite uncomfortable being in court. He always felt an obligation to never discuss his patient's cases with anyone other than their immediate family. Today, he was being asked to disclose Mrs. Olson's condition to the whole world.

He took his oath and sat in the witness stand.

Ethan approached and addressed him, "Dr. Woods,

would you please tell the court about your qualification, profession and relation with Mrs. Olson?"

Dr. Woods gave the details of his medical degree and his professional experience to the court. He then went on to say, "Mrs. Olson is my patient. She was diagnosed with dementia over two years back. She has been under my care ever since."

"Can you please share with the court some details about Mrs. Olson's mental condition?" enquired Ethan.

"Well, she often experiences memory loss, disorientation, mental confusion, and hallucinations among other things," replied Dr. Woods, reluctantly.

Ethan was not going to let go yet. He asked, "Has her condition improved over time?"

Dr. Woods hesitated as his eyes met those of Mrs. Olson, who was in the public sitting area. He felt bad for his patient. He believed that the key to curing any illness along with medication, was to instill in the patient the belief that they were getting better. 'Nothing works better than self-confidence' was the conviction he always held. Therefore, he had always told Mrs. Olson that she was getting better, so as to help with her recovery. It was now working against her. Mrs. Olson was expecting him to tell the world that she was getting better when it was far from the truth.

Ethan saw the exchange of looks between them and understood the doctor's dilemma. He tried to make the doctor feel better by saying, "I understand your hesitation, doctor. As you are aware, you are here as per your patient's suggestion. Your testimony is important to the case, as it can help keep an innocent man out of prison. Moreover, you are under oath. Please answer the question. Has Mrs. Olson's condition improved over time?"

Dr. Woods avoided looking in Mrs. Olson's direction as he replied in a low voice, "No. It has deteriorated."

There was a loud gasp in the courtroom.

Ethan then asked his most important question. "Dr. Woods, in your professional opinion, having treated Mrs. Olson for over two years for her mental condition, do you think she is fit to testify in court?"

Dr. Woods lowered his eyes and shook his head as he said, "No, she is not."

Mrs. Olson couldn't hold herself anymore. She shouted from the public sitting area, "You liar! You told me I was getting better. Why are you lying now? I might be on medication, but I can tell when my daughter is unhappy. I have told only the truth. I am not crazy!"

The judge asked security to escort Mrs. Olson out of the courtroom to maintain order. Two well-built security guards followed the order while she continued to scream frantically.

Dr. Woods had never felt so helpless in his career. He felt so ashamed seeing Mrs. Olson being dragged out of court because of what he said, that he wanted to quit his medical profession. 'My job was to heal patients, not hurt them,' he thought to himself.

Ethan felt sorry for the old woman, but he cleared his mind and shifted his focus back to the court he had a case to win. He submitted Mrs. Olson's medical file to the court and continued, "As confirmed by Dr. Woods, I request the court to make inadmissible all that she has said in court during the trial."

Judge Nicholas went through Mrs. Olson's medical file. After deliberating on the matter for a moment, he looked at the jury and instructed, "Mrs. Olson's testimony is now inadmissible in court. Hence, you must not consider her earlier testimony. Whatever she has said in court shall not be included as evidence and should not affect the verdict."

The jury made a note.

Liam slumped in his seat, relieved to hear that his mother-in-law's testimony was now inadmissible. He was further relieved as the prosecution would not be able to call her for any further questioning as well.

Jacob looked visibly distraught as Mrs. Olson's testimony had been crucial for the case, but there was nothing he could do about it. He knew he had to move ahead and focus if he was to win the case.

Judge Nicholas then asked Mr. Harris to continue and call upon his next witness.

The prosecution called the defendant, Mr. Montcherry, to the stand. There was a brief murmur in the court. The jury's body language also changed as they sat up with interest to hear the defendant's side of the story. Some members of the jury got ready with their notepad and pens, as if to take notes.

The relief on Liam's face vanished as he felt nervous about being questioned.

Liam walked up to the stand and was sworn in.

Judge Nicholas addressed Liam. "Mr. Montcherry, are you aware that you could refuse to testify at this trial and the jury would not hold it against you?"

"Yes, Your Honor. I am aware and I am willing to testify. I have nothing to hide," Liam confirmed. Ethan had repeatedly advised Liam not to testify, but Liam had insisted, saying that only guilty people don't take the stand and that he wanted to tell his side of the story to the jury.

"Very well then, you may proceed, Mr. Harris," said the judge.

The prosecutor noted how Liam was fidgeting with his wedding ring as he began his questioning, "Mr. Montcherry, can you explain to the court why you were partying with your friends without your wife on the night of your first anniversary?"

Liam was taken aback by the question. This was not on the list of probable questions that Ethan had prepared him for. Nonetheless, he composed himself quickly and said, "I wish every second that I had not left her sleeping that night and gone to my friend's house. We had an amazing day of celebrations that ended with dinner at The Deveraux's, our favorite restaurant. However, Cloe is… I'm sorry, Cloe was… an early sleeper. She was particular about the time she went to bed. She usually slept latest by 10:30 p.m., unless there was an event or a party. Our house help can confirm this. That night, Mathew called me for drinks, and I went to join him and his friends around 11 p.m. Cloe had already slept by 10:30 and I had been watching TV. Besides, this was not the first time I had gone to his house after Cloe slept. She was good with it. It was nothing out of the ordinary."

"Can you explain why Cloe called her mother multiple times that night but didn't make a single call to you? You were her husband; shouldn't she have called you first? She even dialed 911, but not you. Can you explain that?" inquired Mr. Harris, his eyebrows raised.

"I had left my phone at home by mistake. She must've seen it lying there and therefore must have not called my number," Liam replied confidently.

"Now, Mr. Montcherry, when you reached home the next morning, you saw your wife with a pillow on her face. Can you explain why, instead of removing the pillow and trying to give her some kind of first aid, you chose to call 911 and waited for the cops to come first?" questioned Mr. Harris, eyeing him dubiously.

Liam fumbled as he spoke, "Errr… I had had a few drinks and my mind was not functioning well, I think. I was in shock."

Some members of the jury shook their heads in disbelief.

Mr. Harris walked over to the center and said, "Your Honor, as discussed earlier about Liam's alibi, he could have reached home, killed his wife, got the pizza from the gas station, and gone back to the party, all within 45 minutes. As confirmed by witnesses present at Mathew Davis's house and according to the CCTV camera outside his house, Mr. Montcherry left

Mathew's house at 11:30 p.m. and returned at 12:15 a.m. with the pizza. On a late weekday night, one can easily reach the gas station from Mr. Davis's house within ten minutes, which would allow him to reach there by 11:40 p.m. But according to the CCTV footage at the gas station, he arrived there only at midnight."

There was a loud gasp and whispering from the people sitting in the courtroom. There was certainly an unaccounted time lag of twenty minutes between the time of Mr. Montcherry's exit from Mathew's house and his entry into the gas station.

"Maintain order," announced the judge. The murmur died, but one could sense the anticipation in the air.

Mr. Harris continued, looking visibly pleased by his argument and the response it got in court. He faced the judge and stated, "I would like to bring to the court's attention that it takes five minutes for him to go to his own house from Mr. Davis's house and another five minutes from his house to the gas station in question. That gives Mr. Montcherry the ten critical minutes that he could have used to kill his wife and also return with the pizza just in time to have an alibi." He then turned to challenge Liam and said, "Isn't that true, Mr. Montcherry?"

"Objection, Your Honor. Badgering," interrupted Ethan.

"Sustained," said the judge.

"Withdrawn," said Mr. Harris.

Mr. Harris again moved his gaze to Liam and

asked, "How would you account for the missing twenty minutes from your trip to get the pizza on the night of the murder, Mr. Montcherry?"

Liam felt cornered by the continuous questioning. He felt beads of perspiration on his forehead. Nonetheless, he tried to keep his cool and replied, "As I left to buy pizza that night, I saw an old man lying on the road in front of my car. He seemed to be injured and in pain. There were marks on his face, and he wasn't being able to get up. He requested me to drop him at the nearest train station, as he wanted to catch the first morning train to Boston. I drove him and dropped him to the station," replied Liam.

"Did anyone see you with the old man? Do you have his contact details, or even his name?" challenged Mr. Harris.

"No, I do not have his name or contact details, as he was not in a position to talk much. I don't think anyone saw me with him. It was late in the night and the roads were deserted," shrugged Liam.

"Mr. Montcherry, your car is seen leaving Mr. Davis's house and then seen arriving 20 minutes later at the gas station in the CCTV cameras. Can you please tell the court how there is no CCTV footage of you or your car for these 20 minutes anywhere in the city of New York? Do you expect the court to believe that you went only by the CCTV blind spots?" demanded Mr. Harris, clearly losing patience.

"That is a mystery to me as well. I am clearly being set up!" shouted a distraught-looking Liam.

"Your Honor, this alibi does not hold good. What I am saying will fit into place, when the autopsy results come in. I am sure the time of murder would tally with those unaccounted twenty minutes. We will then have a clear insight into the cause of Mrs. Montcherry's death," continued Mr. Harris.

Ethan Carson was feeling frustrated as he watched his client's alibi crumble in court. The gap in the CCTV footage of the city was beyond his understanding as well. He took it as a technical glitch, as he could not imagine anyone going to the lengths of tampering with the city's CCTV cameras to set him up. Liam had mentioned about the old man during their discussion on the time gap in his alibi. Ethan had not found it to be convincing enough for the jury, but he had decided to go along with it, as he had felt that he was left with no other option. He had hoped that the prosecution would not notice the tiny 20-minute gap, but to his dismay, his worst nightmare had just come true. As he tried to make eye contact with his client, he noticed Mr. Montcherry had grown pale and nervous.

"Mr. Montcherry, when were you going to inform the court that you had a fifty-million-dollar life insurance policy on Cloe Montcherry?" mocked Mr. Harris.

Liam was flabbergasted. Though Ethan had warned him that prosecution would definitely bring it up, Liam had not believed him.

"Objection, Your Honor. Assuming facts not in evidence," said Ethan. Ethan had to pretend that he was unaware of the policy to avoid a perjury charge against him. Liam gave him an apologetic look as their eyes met.

"Council approach," said the judge.

Ethan and Jacob went close to the judge for a private conversation. Mr. Harris spoke in a soft voice. "Your Honor, it has only now come to my knowledge that the defendant had taken a life insurance policy for the victim. I want to introduce it in court as it could have an impact on the outcome of the case."

Ethan displayed shock and convinced them that he had no prior knowledge of this policy.

The judge looked at the documents and asked Ethan, "Is it okay with you to introduce it today or do you need time?"

With all his experience in the judiciary system, Ethan knew they had this coming and was well prepared for it. He hoped that Liam would recall his prep talk, as he had not taken it seriously then.

Ethan spent a minute going through the insurance papers for effect, so that his excuse of being unaware would look plausible, and then agreed. The judge allowed the insurance policy in court.

"Objection withdrawn, Your Honor," said Ethan as he took his seat.

"Mr. Montcherry, you didn't think we would find out about it, did you?" mocked Mr. Harris, visibly proud of himself.

"All responsible people take out insurance policies. Are they all murderers?" retorted Liam.

"Isn't it too much of a coincidence that you took the policy and within one year, your wife dies?" enquired Mr. Harris.

"Well, my marriage is only one year old, and I took the policy out within a month of us getting married. Besides, I had taken the same policy out for myself as well. It is standard practice in most households in today's uncertain times," reasoned Liam.

"Mr. Montcherry, whatever you say, it does not deny the fact that this insurance money is large enough to qualify as a clear motive for you to kill your wife, right?" exclaimed Mr. Harris.

"Objection, Your Honor. Badgering," interrupted Ethan.

"Sustained," said the judge and warned Mr. Harris.

"Withdrawn," said Mr. Harris. The point was made. He smiled slightly at having successfully planted the information in the jury's mind.

Mr. Harris was not done yet. He continued, "Can you explain why your personal CCTV cameras in and around your house stopped working at the night of the murder? Who could have tampered with the equipment in your private property, Mr. Montcherry?"

Liam lashed out, "I am absolutely clueless! It's all electronic. Anyone can tamper with it from anywhere through the internet. I believe the person who murdered Cloe must have done that as well."

Mr. Harris gave a visibly sarcastic smile while eyeing Liam and said, "No further questions, Your Honor."

Mr. Carson had never lost a case before and was in no mood to make this an exception. He knew he had to do something and do it fast.

He then walked up to the witness stand to cross-examine his client. "Did you love your wife, Mr. Montcherry?" he asked.

"Yes, of course, I did," Liam replied with conviction. "When did you find out that your wife was dead?" asked Ethan.

"Early morning around 6 a.m., when I came back from Davis' house," replied Liam with a sullen face.

"Was the house broken in? Any smashed windows?" inquired Ethan.

"No, there were no signs of forced entry, but the door was unlocked when I reached home," mentioned Liam.

"Who all have keys to your house, Mr. Montcherry?" asked Ethan.

"We have four sets of keys to the house. One each were with Cloe, our live-in staff, and me. The fourth one stays hidden under one of the plants in our garden for emergencies. Cloe followed this practice in all her homes growing up and insisted on keeping one in our house and after marriage, insisted on keeping one in our house too. The killer must have known about this habit of Cloe's and used the key to get in," replied Liam.

"Did you check if the fourth key was still under the plant after the murder?" enquired Ethan.

"The forensic team did look for it, but it has been missing. I am assuming that the killer entered my home using this particular key with ease, without having to break in." replied Liam.

"No further questions, Your Honor," concluded Ethan.

The jury looked confused as they observed Ethan's cross-examination.

"The witness is excused," said the judge.

"Your Honor, the prosecution rests their case," said Jacob, feeling satisfied with his witness line and the response he received for his arguments.

The ball was in Ethan's court now. It was time for him to up his game and win the case, but he almost felt dizzy at the thought of his weak witness lineup as compared to what had just happened in court.

"Is the defense ready with its case?" said the judge, interrupting Ethan's thoughts.

Ethan stood up and replied, "Your Honor, I call the defendant's housemaid, Ms. Mary Alberto, as my first witness."

Ms. Alberto was escorted to the witness stand and sworn in.

Ethan approached the witness stand and began his interrogation. "Ms. Alberto, can you tell the court about how long you have been working at Mr. Montcherry's house?"

"Sir, I was the first-person Mr. Montcherry hired when he moved into the Montcherry Mansion over 10 years ago. I have been there ever since," replied Ms. Alberto.

"How many house helps does the house have now?" asked Ethan.

"Sir, the house currently has three live-in maids and two butlers. The old butler was hired a month after I joined while the other three were hired after Sir's marriage, as more help was needed. Now they don't know if Sir will need them anymore," sobbed Ms. Alberto, feeling concerned about her fellow workers.

Ethan tried to get back to his line of questioning and continued, "How was the couple's mood on the day of the murder, Ms. Alberto? Were there any fights between them on that day?"

"It was their first anniversary. They were both very happy. There were no fights that day as per my knowledge," confirmed Ms. Alberto.

"All right. What did you see on the night that Cloe Montcherry was murdered? Did you notice anything out of the ordinary?" Ethan came to the point.

"They had asked for privacy that evening, as they were celebrating. All the staff, including me, retired for the day at 5 p.m. itself. There was, anyway, no work to be done as they were going out for dinner. Sir, we have no clue about what happened with Madam that night. We came to know only the next morning when Sir ran out calling us." Her face suddenly lost color as she continued, "Madam was so young. That is no age to die. We still cannot believe someone could kill her."

"Is that so? How is it that a murder took place and you heard nothing? Can you tell the court how far your room is from Mr. Montcherry's bedroom?" continued Ethan, trying to make a point to the jury.

"We live in the outhouse, sir, which is about 20

yards away from the mansion. We come to the mansion in the morning and then go back there to sleep when work is done," informed Ms. Alberto.

"Makes sense. Was it out of the ordinary that the couple asked for privacy that evening or was it a regular practice?" asked Ethan.

"It was very normal, sir. They often dismissed us early when they were dining out. At least once a week we were dismissed early," confirmed Ms. Alberto.

"All right. Was it also out of the ordinary that Mr. Montcherry went out partying after Mrs. Montcherry slept, or was it a regular practice as well?" asked Ethan.

"It was nothing out of the ordinary. Madam was into fitness and health and usually slept early. Sir, on the other hand, was used to his late nights. Madam was completely okay with him going out after she slept," confirmed Ms. Alberto.

"Thank you for confirming that Ms. Alberto. Since you have lived with Mr. Montcherry for so long, what can you say about his temperament? Do you feel he has displayed any violent behavior over the years?" asked Ethan.

"Not at all. He always deals with everyone with utmost respect. He has not lost his temper once, even when we staff make mistakes of any kind. Mr. Montcherry is very kind and even-tempered," confirmed Ms. Alberto.

"This clearly proves that the defendant, Mr. Montcherry is a man of mild temperament and is not violent to commit a serious crime as murder. Ms. Alberto has also confirmed that the couple were happy on the day of their anniversary and were celebrating. With my next witness, I will prove to the court that the victim, Cloe Montcherry, had enemies of her own, and the defendant had no motive to kill his loving wife. I have no more questions," Ethan said and then sat down.

Judge Nicholas called out, "Does the prosecution wish to cross-examine?"

"Yes, Your Honor," said Jacob, rising from his seat.

"Ms. Alberto, can you tell us about the relationship between Mr. and Mrs. Montcherry? Did they always seem happy as you testified about their anniversary day? Did they never fight during their one year of marriage?"

"Errrrr, which couple doesn't fight?" said Ms. Alberto, amused by the question.

"Ms. Alberto, I am not asking about other couples. Please stick to answering the questions being asked. You are under oath," said Jacob, trying to intimidate the house help.

Ms. Alberto wrung her hands and then haltingly replied, "As such, they... They were happy with each other. B... But they did fight sometimes."

Jacob then questioned, "Are the house helps aware about the existence and location of the spare key to Mr. Montcherry's house?"

She shook her head in complete confusion and uttered, "There is no spare key to the house. The staff has one common key, and Sir and Madam had the other two."

Jacob then smiled at the jury and concluded by saying, "No more questions."

Judge Nicholas excused the witness and instructed, "You may call your next witness, Mr. Carson."

Ethan got up and replied, "I call Ms. Kelsey Lynskey to the stand."

The witness was bought in and made to take her oath.

Ethan began his questioning, "Ms. Lynskey, would you tell the court about your relationship with the victim?"

Kelsey replied, "I am Cloe's childhood friend. I've also been working with her at her fashion label since its conception."

Ethan nodded and continued, "Can you tell us about Cloe's temperament?"

"She was a sweet and shy girl while growing up. We shared so many fond memories," Kelsey replied in a low voice, as her thoughts wandered to their childhood days.

"How had she been lately, Ms. Lynskey? How was her attitude with her colleagues, staff and partners?" Ethan asked as he tried to bring her back to the present.

Kelsey responded, "Cloe was immensely talented. Fame and success came very early to her. Unfortunately, she had a sudden personality shift as her talent got global recognition. She became very arrogant, and it became tough for people to work with her. Her staff were constantly changing as she openly insulted them."

"Ms. Lynskey, can you think of people in her

professional environment who would be upset enough to want to harm Mrs. Cloe?" asked Ethan.

"I cannot think of any particular names, but there are many. She was very vocal about her displeasure with people and did not think twice before demeaning anyone. She definitely had enemies," confirmed Kelsey.

Ethan smirked as he looked at Jacob and then addressed the court, "Your Honor, it is evident from Ms. Lynskey's testimony that the victim had many enemies at the workplace. The killer could have been someone who had been offended by her."

With that, Ethan ended his questioning. The judge then excused the witness as the prosecution did not want to cross-examine.

Ethan's heart rate increased as he realized he had no more witnesses. He had not expected Liam's testimony to go so terribly. He gazed at the jury in desperation. The jury had not made up their minds about whether or not Liam was guilty, not yet.

To Ethan's relief the judge announced, "Court will resume on Monday. Have a good weekend, everyone." Court was adjourned.

Ethan realized that there was only one way to save his client, and that was to find the killer and produce him or her in court.

Chapter 9

The Trial

Saturday,

Ethan on a Time Clock

Everyone had the weekend off, but Mr. Carson had work to do. His agenda was to find the killer, but he was worried about the limited time he had to accomplish it.

The delayed autopsy report was not helping, either. The medical examiner had been asked to expedite the report as it was critical to the case. Martin was keeping a close tab on the progress and was to inform Ethan as soon as the report was made available.

For the rest of the day, Ethan went through the court's proceedings over and over in his head. He wanted to catch anything important that he may have missed. He went through the case files all over again, keeping in perspective all the new findings that had got revealed during the trial so far. He imagined the many possibilities of who could have been the murderer and re-analyzed the lives of every person the couple knew.

Ethan decided to spend more time on the couple's social media than he had done earlier. He had passed on this task to Martin during their initial investigation phase, but Martin had failed to find anything of significance. Social media was not for him, but Ethan was desperate to find the killer and was in no position to take any chances.

He went over every post, picture, and video the couple had ever uploaded on their social media accounts with a fine-toothed comb. It was the most painstaking task Ethan had ever taken up in his career. 'How could someone be so active on social media?!' he thought to himself as he read post after post on their accounts. Ethan noticed quite a number of negative comments on their posts. Though it was the obvious side effect of being celebrities, he still stalked the profiles of people who had written anything remotely negative on any of their posts. Eventually, he felt completely drained by the exercise and decided to take a break.

He walked to the room of his all-time stress busters. Alexi and Evan were thrilled to see him. They hugged him and told him how much they had missed him. Ethan enjoyed listening to the highlights of their week. They then decided to play their favorite game, 'Laugh Aloud', where all participants told jokes and the joke that got the loudest laugh won. Ethan called for Sienna, and she happily joined them. After around an hour of riotous laughter, Ethan felt refreshed. He kissed his lovely children and beautiful wife as he went back to his study and got to work, feeling relaxed.

Ethan decided to once again watch the CCTV footage from The Deveraux's. He checked the footage from the time Liam and Cloe arrived for dinner to celebrate their first and, unfortunately, last anniversary. He paid close attention as this was just hours before the murder. In the tape, Ethan watched Mr. and Mrs. Montcherry entering the restaurant and immediately being surrounded by fans for pictures. Liam and Cloe obliged them with selfies. The couple seemed to be in a good mood as they walked hand in hand to the reception. After what appeared to be a brief conversation with the lady there, they went to the corner table on the right and sat down. Everything seemed to be normal. After a few minutes of looking at the menu, they called the waiter to take their order. They ordered a fine bottle of champagne to drink along with caviar for Liam and mushrooms for Cloe, as she was a vegetarian. The waiter left to get their order. Ethan closely analyzed every detail in the tape. Soon, the chef came with a bottle of champagne and glasses. He shook hands with Liam, as if congratulating him. He then opened the champagne bottle in style, poured it in their glasses and left. A while later, the waiter came back with the food and served the couple.

Ethan's brows furrowed as a thought cropped up in his mind and he hurriedly checked something on his laptop. Then suddenly, it clicked! Had he really found the killer? Ethan wondered about his good luck and great investigation skills.

Ethan smirked as he felt a sudden respect for technology. Without speaking to a single person, you could dig out every detail about anyone or any place in the world.

He shrugged and immediately called Bryan and gave him the name of the prospective killer he had just discovered. 'I definitely cannot rely on my associate, Martin, for the job,' he thought to himself. Ethan believed in working smart rather than working hard. He sometimes used Bryan's expertise of extracting the life history of people when he had less time at hand. It was, of course, done discreetly, and on his own dime. Bryan assured him that he would have a file on the person first thing in the morning.

Ethan then gave Liam a call and asked him to meet him at The Deveraux's the next day at 3 p.m. Liam sounded frustrated at the way the last hearing had gone and warned him saying the meeting better be productive. Ethan reassured him and hung up.

Ethan went to sleep with a smile, satisfied with the belief that he had got the killer.

Chapter 10

The Trial

Sunday,

Witness Hunting

On Sunday, Ethan got up at 7 a.m. sharp. While getting dressed, he glanced at the sleeping form of his wife. Ever since the trial had begun, he had hardly been with his family. He thought of making it up to them next week as the trial would be over soon. Looking into the mirror while combing his short brown hair, he felt pleased with himself, thinking that he had probably nailed the culprit.

He drove to the nearest Starbucks where he was to meet Bryan. He ordered his favorite white mocha with vanilla syrup and java chips and sat on a corner bench with his laptop. He was enjoying his morning dose of caffeine when Bryan discretely dropped a file on his table and disappeared.

Ethan was impressed as he went through the

contents of the file. It had the prospective killer's life history staring at him. All kinds of records—birth, education, work, relationships, criminal offenses—were neatly compiled and labeled. It had enough evidence to confirm his theory. Ethan was on a mission as he started going through the file. After hours of reading, he felt that he knew the killer like the back of his hand. He pondered over the motive the killer would have had to kill Cloe Montcherry. By the time he was through with his research, it was 2:30 p.m. He knew everything and anything there was to know to nail the real killer.

He called up Martin and shared his theory with him. Martin's respect for Ethan suddenly skyrocketed. He was impressed by Ethan's investigation.

Ethan was a disciplined man and a stickler for punctuality. He respected people's time, and expected the same in return. He drove to The Deveraux's and reached there at 2:58 p.m. for his meeting with Liam and made himself comfortable at the fourth table to the left from the corner.

He then saw Liam Montcherry walking into the restaurant, wearing a blueish-black coat, a red tie, a single wireless earphone, and pitch-black Ray-Ban shades. He walked in style and threw himself on the chair next to Ethan's with total swagger. His demeanor made Ethan wonder, 'Is he even a bit affected by his wife's death? Well, at least he came on time.' He shrugged.

Liam was in a foul mood today and was upset with Ethan. Considering his high legal fees, Liam had expected Ethan to quickly prove him not guilty with his brilliance but, at best, the jury seemed confused to him. Due to this unsatisfactory outcome, he had come to meet him today with great reluctance.

Soon after, a waitress came to the table. "May I get you anything, gentlemen?" she smiled and waited with a tab in her hand, ready to take their order.

"Iced tea for me, and… I'll take a wild guess, water for him," mocked Liam.

"That's right," nodded Ethan, ignoring his sarcasm. He continued, "I would also need you to call Jeffery Crowder. He still works here, doesn't he?" Then, looking at her name tag pinned to her shirt, he smiled and said, "Nice name, Sofia."

"Thank you, and sure, sir. I'll call him right away. Who should I say has come to see him?" asked the waitress.

"Tell him a guy wearing a crisp suit has come to meet him," he replied with a wink and then added with a grin, "I'm a lawyer." The waitress gave a tiny chuckle and went on her way.

"Jeffery, huh… Who the heck is that douchebag?" asked Liam with irritation in his voice.

"He's the dude who's gonna save you from going to prison. So shut your mouth and let me do the talking," Ethan lashed out. He was done with Liam's attitude!

Liam was taken aback and retaliated. "Hey! You're my lawyer, you don't get to speak to me like that!" He composed himself a bit and then inquired, "All right, how is this guy gonna save me from prison? I don't know any Jeffery Crowder. How is he even related to the case?"

"He's the killer of your deceased wife. If it's not him, well, then it's *you*." Ethan glared at him, keenly observing his expression to evaluate his reaction.

"What? How dare he! My poor Cloe, why did he do that?" said Liam as he got up from his seat, visibly agitated.

"Listen, he is innocent until proven guilty. If you want him behind bars, you keep quiet and let me do the talking. I have got you here so you can observe him and try to recall if you have seen him anytime earlier," Ethan said, trying to put sense into Liam and get him to sit down. Ethan then continued, as calmly as he could, "My job is to prove you as not guilty, and that's what I'm doing. Now, if I can please continue to do my job."

"All right, you do your job," nodded Liam and sat down.

At that moment, the waitress reappeared at their table. She put down a glass of water and a glass of Diet Coke on the table and informed them, "Jeffery Crowder will be with you soon," and walked away.

Liam and Ethan sat there, waiting for the mysterious Jeffery Crowder. After a few minutes, Mr. Crowder came towards their table.

"Good afternoon, fellas. What can I do for y'all?" he Inquired with a smile.

He then looked surprised as he noticed Liam and said, "Good afternoon, Mr. Liam." Liam was a celebrity and was used to being recognized. Ethan observed that Liam had a lost expression on his face, as if trying to place Jeffery.

"We wanted to ask a few questions. It will take only a few minutes," said Ethan.

"Ah, sure. Glad to help," replied Jeffery. Though he appeared to be a bit apprehensive, he obliged. He was obligated to adhere to the unwritten rule of the fine dining restaurant of being helpful to their customers in all ways possible.

Ethan pointed to the empty chair nearby and gestured him to join them at their table.

Jeffery suddenly looked happy, as the rich and elite had never asked him to sit with them before. He pulled up the chair to their table and took a seat, feeling important and ready to help.

"Thank you, Jeffery. However, I'm afraid this isn't small talk. You're a suspect in a murder case," Ethan said sternly.

Ethan watched Jeffery's proud smile drain from his face.

Jeffery sat there in shock and stared into oblivion for a whole minute, as the full implication of the statement hit him. He wanted to run away but sat there, frozen in shock. "Oh! Bu… But I ain't murdered no one! What's the case here?" inquired a jittery Jeffery, looking genuinely confused.

"You must have read or seen in media that Liam's wife is dead," said Ethan.

"Yes, yes, that's all fine, but how do I come into picture?" asked Jeffery.

"Do you not see the connection now?" demanded Ethan.

"Nnnooo… Not at all, I only know what is said in the media, sir," Jeffery faltered, his voice choked with tears.

"Jeffery, let me remind you of a small detail that you seem to be forgetting. His wife, a.k.a. the woman who was murdered, was Cloe Montcherry, and her maiden name was Cloe Olson. Do you see the connection? She was your ex-girlfriend, wasn't she?" smirked Ethan.

Jeffery was dumbstruck as he understood what he was being accused of. He could barely speak properly or move but somehow managed to make words come out of his mouth and stammered, "Bu-bu-but we were not in touch, w-we-we broke up a long time back, been around two years! W-wh-why would I kill her?" It worried him immensely, thinking about what would happen next and if they would send him to prison for murder.

Liam looked shocked and heartbroken at the same time by the revelation. "It's my fault. I realize now how little I tried to learn about my wife's past. I had fallen head over heels in love with Cloe when we first met. I was always only interested in our future together; her past never really mattered to me. I had no idea about Cloe's past relationships!" exclaimed Liam, overwhelmed with emotions and regret.

Ethan gestured Liam to stop talking, to which Liam nodded and kept quiet.

"I saw you on the CCTV footage. Cloe and Liam had come to this restaurant for their anniversary dinner. You were on duty then. You fetched her drink and served her, didn't you? She died within hours of having that drink. This is a bit too much of a coincidence," elaborated Ethan.

"N-no sir, I'm not a murderer. I-I swear I ain't ever killed nobody!" stammered Jeffery.

"Listen, Jeffery. I am Ethan Carson. Liam's lawyer. Now, be ready to come to court on Tuesday. You will be subpoenaed. My associate will get in touch with you with the details," informed Ethan.

Ethan then walked out, leaving some bills to take care of the tab, without glancing back. Liam followed.

Jeffery was sweating like a pig. Sofia found him standing rooted as she came to clear the table. She shook him gently and inquired, "All okay? Did you see a ghost? Why are you looking pale and disturbed?"

Jeffery was now visibly shaking and fumbled, "I… I'm not feeling well. I think I'll take the rest of the day off." He hurried away.

Liam caught up with Ethan as they were walking out. Ethan tried to console a perplexed-looking Liam and said, "I told you, Liam, you are in the right hands. Have patience. You will soon be off the hook, and Jeffery will be behind bars. Also, don't blame yourself. Most people don't care about their partner's past relationships."

Liam's confidence in Ethan had been restored as he exclaimed, "Thank you, Ethan. I apologize for having lost my cool with you today. Good job, Mr. Carson."

They shook hands and smiled as they parted ways.

Ethan's thought went back to his observation of Jeffery's expressions. Jeffery looked too confused to be the killer. But Ethan also knew better than to rely just on facial expressions as anyone capable of taking someone's life, was bound to have the ability to put up a good act. He shrugged the thought away.

The only missing piece now was the autopsy report. The entire case depended on it. Ethan had to formulate his next move depending on the autopsy outcome. Since Ethan had seen Timothy's version of the autopsy report, he had based his theory on it. The re-evaluation opened scope for deviation and that had been Ethan's worry.

Just then, Ethan got the call he had been desperately waiting for. It was Martin confirming that the autopsy report was out. 'Is it my lucky day, or what?!' thought Ethan to himself.

The results were going to be a big surprise to everyone following the case, but not for Ethan.

Ethan then asked Martin to prepare the required documentation for the new witness, so that it could be submitted in court the next day. "I want him on the stand on Tuesday," instructed Ethan.

"On it," confirmed Martin as he got to work immediately. One day, he hoped to be as sharp and meticulous as Ethan.

When Jeffery was told about the autopsy report, he was scared out of his wits. He couldn't imagine going to prison. However, he gathered courage, as he realized he could not escape from going to court.

On the other hand, Liam was glad when he came to know of the news.

Jeffery had every right and reason to be scared at that point, and Liam had every right and reason not to be.

With his chin up and chest bursting with pride, Ethan called his managing partner and narrated the new developments. Michelle was elated. 'The Montcherry account is ours for sure,' he thought to himself.

Ethan went to grab another coffee at Starbucks. This time, he needed a strong Americano to process how the new pieces had completed the puzzle perfectly.

On reaching home, Ethan got to formulating his next move. He usually wrote all his court arguments on his laptop days before any trial began. However, the introduction of a new witness in this case, had added to his work. Luckily, the weekend had helped him with the needed time. He hoped that this development would lead him to win the case.

Ethan went to bed relaxed. He loved productive mid-trial weekends.

He felt he was ready to win the case. But was he?

Chapter 11

The Trial

Day 3, Monday, a Turning Point

Mr. Carson woke up on Monday morning, feeling invigorated as he thought about what lay ahead. During the proceedings on Friday, he had felt the case slipping away from his hands. But the entry of Jeffery Crowder had put him back in control.

He reached the court on time along with others. Soon, the judge entered and after the preliminaries, he gave instructions to proceed with the trial.

Without delay, Ethan handed over a file to the bailiff, while the clerk noted down the amended list of witnesses. The file was then passed on to the judge who went through it.

The judge looked at Ethan and stated, "The defense seems to have come up with a new witness."

Ethan stepped in the center and nodded, "Yes,

Your Honor. Since the witness is pivotal to the trial, I would request the court to approve the amended list of witnesses."

The unexpected twist prompted a flurry of comments amongst the spectators while Jacob looked astounded. The jurors also exchanged inquisitive glances. The judge demanded order in court and said, "Counsel approach."

Both the attorneys moved forward after which the judge divulged the details. Jacob was surprised as he had assumed his victory after Friday's proceedings.

The judge inquired, "Does the prosecution require time to prepare for the new witness?"

Jacob quickly composed himself and said with confidence, "Yes, Your Honor, but I don't need more than a day to understand the new witness. We can continue tomorrow morning."

The judge noted that down while the attorneys returned to their place.

Judge Nicholas then announced, "In light of the new witness, Jeffery Crowder, coming into the picture, and the prosecution needing time for the same, we shall continue with the proceedings tomorrow, that is Tuesday morning. Meanwhile, I shall issue the orders to subpoena the witness." He continued with the formalities of introducing the new witness in the middle of a trial.

Ethan looked supremely confident but was surprised to see Jacob's stoic face. He had expected Jacob to be shaken and perplexed at the introduction of the new witness. Jacob, however, looked neither harrowed nor confident.

The crowd dissipated, abuzz with speculations about the new witness. Everyone was especially curious because the defense attorney had termed him as being 'pivotal' to the trial.

"It has been brought to my attention that the autopsy report has arrived. It will be discussed in the next hearing as well." concluded the judge. Court was then adjourned for the day.

Chapter 12

The Trial

Day 4, Tuesday, The New Witness

All concerned parties assembled at court once again on Tuesday morning. The judge told everyone to be seated and began proceedings for the day.

"Your Honor, I would like to call upon my next witness, Dr. Evelin Jones, the forensic pathologist who has performed the autopsy on the victim," replied Ethan.

The bailiff escorted Dr. Jones to the witness stand and the oath was taken. Ethan informed the court about his professional qualifications and his relevance and eligibility to testify in court.

He then began with his questioning, "Dr. Jones, I will ask straightforward questions."

Ethan paused for dramatic effect, looking around to be sure he had everyone's attention. He then said in a loud voice, "Can you tell the court about the cause of death?"

"The cause of death is poisoning," answered Dr. Jones.

There was a loud murmur in the courtroom as the information sunk in.

Ethan looked at the jury and said, "We can safely assume that placing the pillow on the face of the victim by the killer was only to mislead the investigation."

The murmur now grew louder.

"Order in my court!" demanded the judge.

"Can you tell the court about the time of death and the time of poisoning, Dr. Jones?" continued Ethan as the murmur subsided.

"The time of death was found to be between 11 p.m. and midnight. The time of poisoning would have been between 7 p.m. and 10 p.m.," replied the doctor.

"Thank you, Dr. Jones. We can now say that the victim could have been poisoned at any time during her dinner at the restaurant that fateful night. The prosecution may argue that time of death coincides exactly with the 20-minute window of the defendant's alibi that night. But it is important to note that the 20-minute window coincides with the time of death, not with the time of poisoning. The victim was poisoned hours before the 20-minute window."

Ethan felt relieved with his argument and concluded saying, "No more questions."

"Would you like to cross-examine, Mr. Harris?" asked the judge.

"No, Your Honor," replied Jacob. The autopsy result was straightforward, there was nothing to argue about it. Jacob felt foolish for not having trusted the earlier autopsy report that clearly mentioned poisoning as the cause of death just because the report was made by Ethan's best friend. He got blinded by the pillow kept on the victim's face and assumed Ethan was trying to cover up death by suffocation. The 20-minute window in Liam's alibi coinciding with the victim's 911 call had seemed like too much of a coincidence to him then.

Judge Nicholas then continued, "The autopsy report has been noted. The defense may call upon its new witness."

"Defense calls Mr. Jeffery Crowder," announced Ethan, feeling pleased with himself.

Mr. Crowder was summoned. After he had taken his oath, he settled on the witness stand, sitting on the edge, apprehensive about the proceedings.

Ethan then walked up to question him, "Mr. Crowder, I will ask direct questions, as I don't want to waste the court's time. Are you the victim, Cloe Montcherry's ex-boyfriend?"

"Yes, sir. I was her ex-boyfriend," replied Jeffery.

"When did your relationship end? Who was the one to end it?" asked Ethan.

"We broke up around two years back. Uh… She was the one who broke up with me, and gradually, I moved on," replied Jeffery. He managed to keep a straight face, though the beads of perspiration on his forehead and the quiver in his voice gave him away.

"Mr. Crowder, would you care to tell the court where you work and in what capacity?" questioned Ethan.

"I work at The Deveraux's as a chef," mumbled Jeffery, knowing what was coming to hit him next.

"I would like the court to note that this is the same restaurant that Mr. and Mrs. Montcherry went to for their first anniversary dinner, just a few hours before Mrs. Montcherry's death," said Ethan while turning to face the jury.

"Is it true, Mr. Crowder, that you prepared the drink for Mrs. Montcherry that evening?" demanded Ethan in a high-pitched voice to get the complete attention of everyone present in the courtroom.

Jeffery screamed agitatedly, like it was the last chance he was getting to convey his side of the story to the court. "*Noooo!* I ain't the person who prepared her drink. I only poured the champagne into their glasses. Mr. Montcherry is fit and healthy even though the drink was poured from the same damn bottle. The two drinks were from the same bottle! How can y'all say that one gal died after having my drink while this guy is absolutely fine?"

There was complete silence in the courtroom as everyone was processing the scenarios being discussed.

However, Ethan was unperturbed. "Mr. Crowder, were you the one who got the glasses for the couple?"

"Yea, I got the glasses and the champagne bottle but that doesn't mean anything," defended Jeffery.

"Your Honor, the poison need not have been in

the champagne. It may have been in the glass. That is why, it is completely possible that the same drink was poured for two people and only one was affected with the poison," explained Ethan, looking at the judge and the jury.

The jury seemed to be in agreement, as there were some nods.

"You are a chef at the restaurant. Why were you the one to serve the drinks? Was there a shortage of waiters at a famous fine dining restaurant like The Deveraux's"? continued Ethan.

"It was the wedding anniversary of Mr. and Mrs. Montcherry. It's standard practice for the chef to meet and congratulate high-profile guests celebrating any occasion," informed Jeffery.

"Can you recall where Cloe kept the spare key to her house while you dated her?" enquired Ethan.

"Of course. She used to call it my key. It was always kept under the plant in front of her house," replied Jeffery, without understanding the implication of his answer.

There was a gasp from the public, and the jury seemed shocked at this new finding.

"That is right. You knew well of her habit of keeping the spare key of her house under a plant, making it convenient for you to enter her current home," said Ethan, feeling proud about the way he had managed to trap Jeffery.

"I did not know it was still her habit," said Jeffery,

feeling stupid for not answering questions to his advantage.

"Can you tell the court where you were between 7 p.m. and midnight on the night of the murder?" enquired Ethan.

"I was at the restaurant from 7 p.m. to 10 p.m. Then my shift got over and I went home and slept," replied Jeffery with conviction.

"Can anyone vouch for you sleeping at home after you left the restaurant?" asked Ethan.

"Why would someone watch me sleep?" asked Jeffery in disbelief.

There was laughter in the courtroom. Jeffery was clearly not used to courtroom questioning.

The judge demanded order in his court and asked Ethan to continue.

"Mr. Crowder, I have one last question for you. Are you active on social media?" asked Ethan.

"Yes, very much. Social media is like breathing for our generation. I am very active," said Jeffery confidently.

"Then please tell the court why you still have your pictures with your ex-girlfriend on your social media? In fact, if it weren't for those pictures, I wouldn't have been able to connect you to this murder in the first place!" exclaimed Ethan.

Jeffery had never felt this bad about being disorganized before. "Okay, so I forgot to delete her pictures and poured her drink, but I didn't kill nobody! Please, y'all, don't send a man to prison for a deed he ain't done," pleaded Jeffery in a wobbly tone.

The silence in the courtroom was thick with suspense as everyone listened intently.

Mr. Carson paced near the jury box and said, "Your Honor, Mr. Crowder does not have an alibi for the night of the murder. His motive here is also crystal clear. The victim broke up with the witness and humiliated him. He did not get over her, as can be concluded from the pictures of Cloe on his social media. When he saw her happy and celebrating with her new love, he got triggered and decided to kill her to get back at her. He first poisoned her drink at the restaurant. He then went to the couple's home and waited till Liam was gone and entered the house with the spare key. He made doubly sure that the victim died by trying to suffocate her under a pillow. He confirmed having knowledge of the spare key location. Mr. Crowder here has poisoned and killed the victim, the motive clearly being revenge!"

Jacob had been raging all this while, feeling despaired as he realized how convincing the defense argument appeared.

"Objection, Your Honor. Council is testifying," said Mr. Harris, interrupting Ethan.

"Sustained, Mr. Carson," said the judge, strictly eyeing Ethan.

"Withdrawn," said Ethan.

Suddenly someone's phone rang, breaking everyone's attention from the case.

Ethan was bugged by the disturbance. 'Who could have brought their phone to the courtroom?' he thought. He was disappointed when he saw his associate disconnecting a call. Ethan wondered what Martin had learned at Harvard. It's basic to keep your phone on silent mode in the courtroom.

The phone rang again, and Martin quickly disconnected it once again.

There was then a series of rapid beep sounds from the phone. Ethan hurried to his associate and uttered, "Better switch off your phone, Martin!"

To his astonishment, Martin whispered, "Ethan, it's your phone, not mine."

Ethan realized he must have forgotten to put his phone on silent mode when he had entered the courtroom this morning.

The judge looked at Ethan and mocked, "Looks like someone really needs you, Mr. Carson. Just take the damn call. The court is adjourned for 30 minutes. We can all do with some air. Everyone, please return on time."

Just then, his phone rang again. Ethan quickly took the call this time as he stepped out of the courtroom. He listened to his managing partner, Michelle Bennett, speaking at the other end of the phone for a couple of seconds. He rolled his eyes and said with frustration, "Why do people think I want to know everything about everybody?! I am in a courtroom, for God's sake!" Ethan disconnected the call and came back into the courtroom, visibly irritated with his managing partner for disturbing him for an irrelevant reason when she knew he was in the middle of an important trial.

The judge returned on time and the proceedings continued.

Ethan apologized for the interruption and then continued, "I have no further questions, Your Honor," he walked back to his seat and sat down.

Ethan's mind wandered to the time he was going through the CCTV footage of the restaurant Mr. and Mrs. Montcherry had gone to for dinner. He was glad that he had gone through social media accounts of not only all of the couple's acquaintances, but also of every person Cloe had come in contact with on the day of her murder. Seeing Cloe's picture with the chef on the chef's social media had alerted him. He trusted his friend Timothy's autopsy report that had been rejected by the prosecution. It had helped Ethan connect the dots, as he was able to establish a link between Jeffery and the case. Timothy's report and the new autopsy report both concluded that poisoning was the reason for Cloe's death. This supported Ethan's theory about Jeffery poisoning Cloe's drink. It was all working well in his favor.

Mr. Harris came forward to cross-examine the witness, with the judge's permission. He began by asking, "Mr. Crowder, were you over your relationship with the victim, Mrs. Montcherry?"

"Uh.. Umm... Yea, I would say I was over my relationship with Cloe," replied Jeffery.

"Did you have any other relationship after your breakup with her?" continued Mr. Harris with his questioning.

"I've had two relationships after our breakup... Uh...

Yea, I have a girlfriend. Her name is Clair Rosewood," replied Jeffery.

Mr. Harris began, "Your Honor, the witness is clearly over his relationship with the deceased. He has been in multiple relationships post his breakup and is still in one. There would be no reason for him to murder his ex-girlfriend after around two years of their break-up. He seems too busy living and enjoying his own life. Moreover, his fingerprints were not found anywhere at the murder scene."

He paused a little for his words to sink in with the jury and then continued, "I have no further questions."

"Your Honor, request to re-examine," said Ethan.

"Go ahead, Mr. Carson," said the judge.

Ethan then faced Jeffery. "So, Jeffery, can you let us know how and why Cloe broke up with you?"

Jeffery uttered, "Well, we were attending a friend's party. O'er there, Cloe heard a rumor about me, but it was all a big misunderstanding! She didn't listen to whatever I had to say and…"

Ethan raised his brows and insisted, "And what, Mr. Crowder?"

Jeffery muttered, "And she slapped me in front of everyone and left the party!"

Ethan shook his head and commented, "Oh! You must have felt embarrassed, being insulted in front of your friends like that!"

"Of course! How dare she slap me in front of so

many people?!" Jeffery shouted in anger. He recalled the insult he had faced and how people made fun of him for months for being slapped by his girlfriend in the middle of a party.

"There you go. The slap may have happened two years back, but your wound is still fresh, like it happened yesterday," said Ethan, pleased with himself for having successfully provoked Jeffery into showing his anger in court.

Jeffery kept his head lowered and didn't reply.

Ethan then turned towards the judge and said, "Your Honor, Mr. Crowder may have moved on. But that does not mean he was able to overcome the resentment he would have felt upon seeing Cloe, happy with her husband. Considering how they had broken up, and how Cloe had publicly humiliated him, he was bound to have felt the urge to avenge himself."

There was no way Ethan would have missed an opportunity this big. He had anticipated Jacob's question and had prepared his reexamining to be able to end with an impact. He knew that he had been able to sow the seeds of doubt in the minds of the jury. All he needed was a reasonable doubt, or was it?

"No more questions, Your Honor," concluded Ethan.

"Is there any further evidence or witness to be presented to the jury?" inquired the judge.

"Your Honor, the defense rests," said Ethan.

"All right, then. You may proceed with the closing

arguments tomorrow. The court is adjourned for the day," concluded the judge.

Both parties had done all they could to present their case to the best of their abilities.

Ethan was especially satisfied about being able to link the murder to Jeffery. He felt he got lucky with the timely finding. With the cause of death being poisoning, it made sense that an ex-boyfriend chef could have poisoned the victim.

Before going to bed, Ethan prepared his closing argument, and set out his clothes for the next day; for it was all that could be done for now.

Chapter 13

The Trial

Day 5, Wednesday, Closing Arguments

Today was the fifth and hopefully the last day of the trial. All concerned parties assembled at court once again. The twelve members of the jury were brought and sworn in.

The judge asked everyone to be seated as he went on to address the jury. "Both the prosecution and the defense have rested their cases. All evidence has been presented in court. Today, each side will make their final arguments about what conclusions you might draw from the evidence. I instruct you to remember that the closing arguments of the attorneys, like their opening statements, are not evidence. However, do listen closely, as they are intended to aid you in understanding the case better."

The jury nodded in agreement.

The judge turned to the attorneys and spoke. "You may proceed with your closing arguments. Now, lawyers, you're not new to court; remember, the prosecutor first, and then the defense."

Mr. Harris came and stood in front of the jurors. He began, "Thank you, Your Honor. Ladies and gentlemen of the jury, thank you for your service. You heard how the defendant left his wife on their first anniversary night to be with his friends. You saw how his wife chose to call her mother when in danger, and not the defendant. You saw how the victim's 911 call was not allowed to go through, and how her phone was smashed. You witnessed the defendant's alibi crumble in court with the lack of CCTV footage backing his story of helping an old man. Also, there was no one else's fingerprints found at the murder scene other than those of the house staff, who have a solid alibi, and of Mr. Montcherry, who has an unexplained 20-minute window in his alibi. You saw how the defendant's 20-minute window in his alibi not only coincides with the victim's calls to her mother and 911 but also the time of death mentioned in the autopsy report. And not to forget, his motive being the 50-million-dollar life insurance policy taken out by him for his wife. Hereby, the prosecution has proved that Liam Montcherry is guilty of murdering his wife in cold blood. Thank you."

To Ethan's horror, the jury looked completely convinced by the prosecution's argument. Most of the members of the jury nodded as if in agreement. Martin exchanged a nervous look with Ethan.

The judge then announced, looking at Ethan, "Defense, you may proceed with your closing argument."

Mr. Carson then stood up, straightened his back and faced the jurors. Intending to persuade them one last time, he said, "Thank you, Your Honor. Ladies and gentlemen of the jury, the prosecution has failed to prove that Mr. Liam Montcherry is guilty. The defendant is devastated with his wife's death. We have proved that it was nothing out of the ordinary for the defendant to visit his friends after the victim slept. He also has an alibi for the night of the murder. The 20 minutes that the prosecution calls a *window* in the alibi is *no window*. Mr. Montcherry was helping an old, injured man at the time. Moreover, the 20 minutes coincides with the time of death, and not with the time of poisoning. It is important to note that the cause of death is poisoning, and it takes time for the poison to take effect. The insurance policy was taken within a month of their marriage. The same policy was taken for the defendant as well. All it proves is that the Montcherrys were responsible people. I would now like to bring your attention to Mr. Jeffery Crowder. The defense has successfully proved that Mr. Jeffery Crowder has a clear motive for killing the victim. His agitation in court during his testimony has proved that his anger towards the victim is very much alive. Mr. Crowder gave the victim a drink, and the victim died due to poisoning a few hours later. This has been supported by the autopsy result as well. He knew the location of the spare key. He could have used the spare key to complete the job instead of completely relying on the poison. The victim would have woken up and on seeing him, would have called her mother and 911. That is when he would have smashed the phone and tried to suffocate her with the pillow. This explains the pillow on the victim's face. As far as the lack of Mr. Crowder's fingerprints at the crime scene is concerned, he could have used gloves so as to leave no evidence behind. Considering the circumstances and evidence, you must find my client, Mr. Liam Montcherry, not guilty. Thank you."

The judge then went on to inform the jury, "Ladies and gentlemen of the jury, now that you have heard the evidence and the arguments, I will inform you about your available legal options that will help you in the jury room. The decision you reach in the jury room must be unanimous. You will never have to explain your verdict to anyone. It will be the foreperson's duty to sign the verdict form once you decide on a verdict."

The judge told them about what the prosecution had to prove if they were to find the defendant guilty. He then went on to remind them that if they were not sure whether Liam Montcherry was guilty, they must find the defendant, not guilty.

Before asking the jury to retire to the jury room, the judge gave them one last instruction. "If you try this case according to the oath which you have taken as jurors, without fear, prejudice, bias or sympathy, you will arrive at a true and just verdict. The bailiff will now escort you to the deliberation room."

The bailiff took the verdict form from the judge and escorted the jury as they retired to make their decision. The remaining concerned people in the courtroom also left and waited in anticipation for the jury to return with a verdict.

Chapter 14

The Trial

Day 5, Wednesday, Hung Jury (Or Not)

The jury room was abuzz. After all, 12 members of the jury settled down, the jury foreperson, Mrs. Gardner read the charge. The members discussed over and over till they understood all facets of the case.

The man with the plaster, Mr. Taylor Davis, happened to be a social media addict and usually posted almost every hour about what he was doing. He was almost having separation anxiety as he had not looked at his social media since the trial. He argued with the others, "In my entitled opinion, since Jeffery had confirmed during his testimony that he was an 'active' social media user and still hadn't removed pictures of his ex-girlfriend from his profile, he was clearly not over her. No active person will forget such a delete. It's standard practice that when you end a relationship, you delete pictures of your ex. Also, she was the one who broke up with him, and that too, with a slap. With his outburst in court, it is clear that he still has feelings for the victim. This gave Jeffery a clear motive and is undoubtedly the killer."

Most of the younger members agreed with him. They acknowledged that in all their past relationships, they had always remembered to remove their ex's pictures, and so did their ex. Meanwhile, the older members felt they did not have the necessary expertise on this matter and stayed neutral on the point.

"But Jeffery's fingerprints were not found anywhere at the crime scene. How could he have entered the house, tried to kill the victim with a pillow, smashed a phone, and not left a single trace of evidence," countered a member, looking visibly proud of his deduction.

"Well, didn't you hear the defense lawyer mention about the killer wearing gloves? Moreover, there are ways to wipe prints after committing a crime. I have watched enough crime documentaries and can vouch for that for sure," said a female member mockingly.

One of the members argued, "50 million dollars in insurance money was motive enough for Liam to kill his wife. I don't know why this is even up for discussion! It's obviously Liam who killed his wife. You don't know to what extent people go to for money nowadays."

The younger generation countered this, saying it was normal practice to take out an insurance policy once one settled down, got married, and became responsible. "I took an insurance policy out for my mother and myself a few weeks back. If my mother got murdered, God forbid, would I automatically be the murderer? I don't believe so. Everyone takes out insurance policies nowadays," argued one of the young men.

One of the women scowled, "Liam left his sleeping wife to party on their first wedding anniversary. That's proof enough that he did not love his wife. Like, what kind of a man leaves his wife on their first wedding anniversary? The answer is nobody, or at least not someone who is supposed to love his wife dearly. He obviously didn't care one bit about her, and all he wanted to do was get himself an alibi by being at his friend's house." The lady's contempt for Liam's lack of sentiment for Cloe was unmistakable.

Another young member countered, "People have different habits, and Liam already said she was a disciplined early sleeper and did not mind him having late nights after she slept. The house help has confirmed that it was nothing new. So, what if it was their anniversary? What was Liam supposed to do? Turn down a party with his friends just to watch his wife sleep? Hard pass," he shrugged, eyeing the lady. Others nodded in favor of the young man.

"Well, none of that matters. Liam's alibi was broken as him, helping the old man could not be proved through the CCTV footage in the area. In fact, there is no footage of him anywhere in the city for the 20 minutes. That's hard proof. No way did he manage to use all the blind spots of the cameras without a meticulous plan," retorted the young man.

To this, the other old lady countered, "Technology cannot decide the fate of a person. You can't convict a man just because he was tryin' to help someone out and technology wasn't able to catch it on camera." She was visibly irritated with the new technology that made her feel old when she was with her children and grandchildren.

"Mrs. Olsen did say that they had a fight before the night of the murder..." began a young man.

"*Heyyy!* Her testimony is not to be considered," interrupted another person.

"Yeah, the judge had revoked her testimony, and we must not think along those lines. The court had declared her unfit to testify," agreed Alyssa.

"We must believe in the court's judgement," nodded Mr. Davis, the man in the cast.

"Well, since there is no more evidence to discuss, let us all start voting, shall we?" suggested Mrs. Gardner, the foreperson. The rest of the jury nodded in agreement.

They then had a round of voting to decide if Liam was guilty as charged or not guilty. It was completed with 100 percent participation.

As they finished voting, the result pointed towards a hung jury. They were divided on the verdict and were unable to reach the required unanimity. The jury members felt very uncomfortable with the outcome.

Mr. Davis addressed the other members, "I have read that a hung jury usually results in the case being tried again."

Alyssa nodded, "Yes, it leads to a mistrial. Guys, this is the first time I'm a part of the jury, and I wish to be amongst the team that brings justice. Let's all re-vote and try to come to a unanimous agreement. We have a duty, let's fulfill it."

Mrs. Gardner suggested, "I think we should have another round of discussion to get some more clarity and try to get to a clean verdict. We can do better than this."

Everyone readily agreed, and they started their discussion from scratch. There was circumstantial evidence against Liam Montcherry, but there was also enough circumstantial evidence against Jeffery Crowder. Both the defendant and Jeffery appeared to have had clear motives as well. Ethan had successfully made it seem like a choice between Liam and Jeffery, though it was only Liam that was being tried for murder.

The jury reflected on what the judge had advised them to do and what their available options were. They made a re-vote, and this time, the jury seemed happy with the outcome. Mrs. Gardner duly noted down each juror's verdict on the verdict form and signed it.

"So, I guess the decision has been made," said Taylor to the rest of the members.

Everyone nodded, as Mrs. Gardner rang the buzzer. In a moment, the bailiff came and escorted them to the courtroom.

Chapter 15

The Trial

Day 5, Wednesday, The Verdict

The courtroom was packed as the jury returned. A large number of journalists had gathered outside the court, competing against each other as always for the news in demand: the verdict. They had a side bet going as to which TV channel amongst them would report the verdict first.

Judge Nicholas asked the foreperson of the jury, Mrs. Clarisse Gardner, to stand. "Have you reached a verdict?" he inquired.

Mrs. Gardner stood up and nodded, "Yes, Your Honor."

The judge asked the defendant to stand and both Liam and Ethan did so.

The judge focused back on the foreperson, Mrs. Gardner, and said, "You may read the verdict."

All eyes were on the old lady as she took the form in her hand and read from it.

Mrs. Gardner began, "We find the defendant, Mr. Liam Montcherry..." and looked around. At this point, the crowd was eager, while Liam and Jeffery were sweating from head to toe. The attorneys held their breath in anticipation. There was immense tension in the room. The old lady then continued, "...Not guilty!"

Liam collapsed in his chair with relief! This had been too close.

Martin shook Ethan's hand with respect.

In order to ascertain that the verdict was unanimous, the judge inquired, "So say you all?" The jurors responded in unison, "Yes, Your Honor."

Mr. Harris looked at the jury in shock. He was known for presenting solid evidence in his cases. However, somehow, he had failed to get enough evidence in this case. He shut his eyes as the words resonated in his mind. 'The defendant is innocent unless the prosecution proves him/her to be guilty beyond a reasonable doubt.' The defendant got the benefit of a lack of concrete evidence against him. The jury did not even consider the large number of circumstantial evidence he had presented. Mr. Harris was visibly disappointed. His thoughts were interrupted by the judge's voice.

"Mr. Montcherry, as per the jury's decision, you are acquitted and free to go," Judge Nicholas said, while looking at Liam. He then glanced at the jurors and concluded, "Thank you, jury, for your time and service."

The prosecutor and Judge Nicholas then spoke about Jeffery Crowder being the new suspect for the murder of Mrs. Cloe Montcherry and discussed the details of the process to initiate proceedings against him.

As people started leaving the courtroom, Jeffery sat there feeling helpless as his worst fears seemed to have come true.

Ethan was in a jubilant mood as he waded through the large crowd and avoided the media gathered outside. He managed to get into his car as he nodded and acknowledged all the congratulations the crowd bestowed upon him. He had done a spectacular job and had once again lived up to his reputation.

Later that night, Ethan had plans with his family. They were elated by his win, and they heard all about the trial from Ethan over a game of Scrabble. The family shared some well-deserved time together after Ethan's hectic work schedule over the past weeks.

Ethan and his wife, Sienna, enjoyed a perfect date night after putting their kids to bed. It was their ritual, of sorts, post every win. He always celebrated his wins with his wife with a date night at home.

Liam was now free and Ethan was still the invincible number 1 attorney.

Chapter 16

Life Goes On

Around three weeks after the final hearing, Ethan was having dinner with his wife. While enjoying some red sauce pasta, he was interrupted by a notification on his phone. It read that his train to the Mexico border was on schedule and was to depart in two hours. He was very confused at this point, and put in his password to enter into his phone. He wanted to check out the app that gave him the notification and was mysteriously downloaded on his phone in the first place. However, his password failed to unlock it. Ethan now broke into a sweat, perturbed by the thought that he had been hacked! He tried his password one more time, but it didn't work. He quickly restarted his phone and tried again, but his password still didn't work. Then, in an attempt to figure out the problem, he removed the pitch-black cover of his phone. To his shock, *the picture of his family he kept in there at all times wasn't there!*

Suddenly, it hit him; it hit him bad. It was Liam's phone! Not his! They both had the same phone and the same cover! They had even joked about having the same boring black cover over the same phone and the chances of their phones getting exchanged. He recollected how they had sat in his office earlier that evening to discuss his pending fees. While conversing, both had kept their mobiles on the table, which is when they probably got exchanged.

He glanced at the mobile once again and wondered, "Why is Liam going to the Mexico border tonight?"

Liam was yet to pay him the larger part of his legal fees. He had informed Ethan that he had received the insurance money a few days back. Liam was scheduled to come to his office the next day to give him the cheque for his pending fees. They even had a lunch planned for the next day. Ethan's mind was once again racing as he tried to make sense of the notification he saw on Liam's phone. He knew that it would take him almost three days to get to Mexico from NYC if he took the train and road route. 'Why not just take a flight, and why the Mexico border?' he wondered. One thing seemed clear to Ethan; this wasn't an unplanned journey.

Ethan was left red-faced as the puzzle pieces moved in his head. "It was Liam who killed his wife, and he is now running away with the money!" Ethan said out aloud, as it clicked. "I will not let him go without paying my legal fees!" he shouted, a nerve ticking in his head. He was not going to let Liam run away!

Ethan got up abruptly, leaving his dinner midway. He called up his associate, Martin, from his landline and asked him to meet him at Liam's house immediately. The associate was almost asleep, but hearing the urgency in Ethan's voice, he sprung out of bed and got into his car.

Sienna was taken aback to see him in this state and inquired about what was happening. Ethan simply shook his head and left in a hurry, saying he would explain later.

Ethan drove at a breakneck speed to Liam's house, trying to catch him before he left for the railway station.

To his horror, when he reached Liam's house, he found the front door wide open. The outhouse, where the servants lived, had a big lock on the door and looked deserted. His associate also arrived just then and parked his car with a screech. He hurried out of his car as he saw Ethan standing by the door of Liam's house. He walked over to Ethan in shock, not able to understand what was going on, as Ethan had not given him the details yet.

"It was him!" Ethan yelled, as the condition of the house proved his worst fear. He rushed into the house to look for Liam, but there was no trace of him. "What do you mean?" shouted Martin, while Ethan checked the house, veranda, and the garage, but they all seemed empty.

Martin started looking for Liam as well. After inspecting a couple of rooms, he climbed up and entered the attic. Everything seemed to be in order, except for a jacket that had been carelessly thrown away in a corner. He found it odd, as the jacket seemed to be in a good condition. Stepping forward, he wondered why anyone would discard it. When he picked it up, something slipped out from its pocket. His face turned pale as he noticed a bottle lying on the floor. *"Ethan!!! Look what I found!!!"* yelled Martin.

Ethan was in the garage. He could hear the urgency in Martin's voice and hurried up to the attic. He saw Martin staring at the bottle and rushed forward. "The poison used to murder Liam's wife!" Ethan exclaimed and shook his head in disbelief.

"Liam must have forgotten about the bottle in this jacket as he fled in a hurry. It is all so clear now. The bottle was not in the house when the crime scene was examined by forensics. The least Liam could have done was destroy it," said Martin as he tried to make sense of what was unfolding before him.

Ethan shrugged. His mind wandered to the same thought he had had while writing his closing argument during the trial: Jeffery wouldn't have risked his perfect poisoning plan by going all the way to Cloe's house just to place the pillow on her face. It now made sense to Ethan. 'It was Liam all along, and now he has fled,' thought Ethan to himself. His thoughts suddenly went to Jeffery. He shuddered as he realized how his reputation was going to be affected when it would be discovered that he had framed the wrong man for murder.

Ethan asked Martin to send the two backup attorneys to the railway station to check on Liam. The attorneys rushed to the station and confirmed that they would call Martin at the sight of Liam.

He thought of informing the police, but he was not sure how it would reflect on the firm if his theory turned out to be wrong. After all, he had based his theory only on the train notification on Liam's phone and his gut.

"Search all areas of the house for any other evidence," ordered Ethan. Martin nodded and began his search.

All Ethan cared about at that very moment was the payment of his legal fees. Liam being the actual murderer or framing the wrong man for the murder were all secondary. He couldn't quite understand why Liam would not pay his legal fees and run away. It wasn't as if he didn't have the money. He was a billionaire, and on top of that, he had 10 million dollars in cash which he had withdrawn after receiving the insurance money. He was in debt to the world and had not been paying his vendors, but he had shown him his financial records. He had enough assets to liquidate which would not only clear his debt but also free him a small fortune. He could very well afford his legal fees, and much more.

'The firm's payment policy is too lenient with celebrity clients; it needs a change right away,' grumbled Ethan. He felt like a fool to have trusted Liam with the payment. Liam was supposed to keep the cheque ready on the day of the verdict, but he asked for an extension till the insurance money came in. Ethan had believed him then, but he now felt that they were all lies.

Truth was the train ticket to the Mexico border! Ethan assumed that Liam would then enter Mexico by road with 10 million dollars in cash! Ethan checked his watch and realized that the train would have already left. He felt miserable about having lost track of time upon the various discoveries at Liam's house.

Ethan felt drained as he entered a dimly lit room. He felt too tired to look for the light switches and decided to sit for a while. He thought of the master switch that hotel rooms had for all the lights in a room, and felt that Liam's huge house definitely needed one. Due to the light in the foyer, he had little visibility and saw a sofa. He rested his hand on the arm of the sofa and was about to sit when he let out a shriek. He felt a sudden sharp pain as a piece of glass pierced his hand. Upon looking closely, he noticed that the sofa was full of broken glass pieces. His gaze then went towards an open door inside the dark room where the lights were switched on. It seemed to be a bathroom. He walked towards the door to wash his wound.

At this point, he wondered, 'If Liam was to flee the country with 10 million dollars in cash, why would he trash the house? Was he trying to show that he had been kidnapped?' Ethan brushed the thought aside as he focused on his bleeding hand.

As he entered the bathroom, he froze in shock. In front of him was Liam's still body in a pool of blood. Liam was dead. "Martin! Get over here *right the hell now*!!" cried Ethan. Martin rushed towards the direction of his voice and entered the bathroom. On seeing Liam's body, it was as if all emotions were sucked out from his face. He stared at the horrific sight.

Ethan's head was reeling now. He was completely baffled and felt disoriented. His entire theory had collapsed.

He rushed out of the bathroom blindly, in a state of panic, and tripped against something. The room started spinning in front of his eyes as he fell and hit his head hard on the floor. He was knocked unconscious.

After what seemed like forever, he woke up to Martin sitting next to him, splashing water on his face. A few minutes had passed since he fell unconscious.

"Are you okay, Ethan?" inquired Martin, his voice full of concern.

Martin had managed to switch on the lights of the room. As Ethan looked around, he noticed the ransacked room; cupboards were emptied, and everything was scattered around. Ethan had thought the mess had been due to Liam leaving in a hurry for the station. He could now see that the place had been trashed. There was glass shattered on the floor and files scattered everywhere. It looked like someone was desperately looking for something.

"I have been thinking while you passed out, Ethan. It has to be Jeffery! He must have killed Cloe, and now he has murdered Liam. It's clearly a lover's spat," explained Martin.

"Jeffery? Yes, you must be right!! That's it! He knows that he is caught and will be going to prison for Cloe's murder anyway. He took advantage of his time out and killed his lover's husband as well," said Ethan, as he shook his head in disbelief.

"But why would Jeffery trash the place, and what is the poison bottle doing in the attic?" asked Ethan, as he gave Martin's theory a second thought.

"Jeffery must have left the poison bottle here to frame Liam. He would have trashed the place to make it look like a random break-in, wherein a thief entered to rob the place and killed Liam during a struggle," said Martin.

"How do you explain the locked outhouse, missing house help, and Liam's train ticket?" asked Ethan.

"Well, I feel Liam must have planned to travel to take a break from all that has happened and would have therefore given leave to his house helps. As for our payment, he would have arranged for someone from his office to give us the cheque tomorrow. He had enough money; we have seen all his documents," explained Martin.

"Right, it all makes sense. We must inform the bureau immediately before Jeffery flees. Give me your phone, Martin," said Ethan. He missed having his own phone since it had all his contact's direct numbers. He knew that his phone would be with Liam, but he did not want to touch the dead body and preferred waiting for the cops to arrive to get it back.

"This is Ethan Carson. Connect me to detective Woods immediately," demanded Ethan.

"Ethan, why aren't you calling on my direct number? Do you want to make me walk to the landline for health benefits?" joked the detective as he spoke on the phone. Over the years, Ethan had built a good rapport with Detective Woods.

"Well, I don't have my phone with me. I'll tell you about it later. It's a long story. First, I have some very important information about Jeffery Crowder," said Ethan with a sense of urgency.

"Oh, news travels fast! I was just leaving for Jeffery Crowder's residence," uttered Woods.

"That's great. I hope you are going to arrest him. What news are you talking about, anyway?" asked Ethan.

"Arrested? He is dead, Ethan," replied the detective, sounding confused.

"Wait! What?!" Ethan was flabbergasted and at a loss of words.

He then got a hold of himself and managed to ask, "How was he murdered?"

"Well, there is no murder. He committed suicide," informed Detective Woods.

"Suicide!" Ethan's mind raced as he thought about the implications. He then almost shrieked with panic, "By any chance, has he left a note or something, confessing to multiple murders?"

"What multiple murders? He has left a note saying he has been wrongly framed for the murder of Cloe Montcherry. It says that he did not commit the crime and that he would rather die than go to prison," said the detective, now confused himself.

"Who lies in their suicide note, detective? He has just murdered Liam Montcherry. In fact, this was the reason for my call—to report Liam Montcherry's murder. My associate and I are at Mr. Montcherry's house right now," informed Ethan.

"What?! I'll dispatch a team to reach there right away. Does the victim's body look like it is rotting in any way?" inquired the detective.

"No, the wound and the blood around looks fresh. Mr. Montcherry may have been shot within the hour or so," replied Ethan.

"Well, then it can't be Jeffery. He died at least three days back. His body had been discovered only this evening, when his neighbors reported a foul smell coming from the house," informed the detective.

Ethan's theory about Jeffery crumbled just as quickly as his theory on Liam had a while back. He was speechless as he hung up the phone.

Martin listened intently as Ethan quickly narrated the details of his conversation with Woods.

They sat on the floor, bewildered, as they waited for the police to arrive.

Ethan then suddenly recalled the phone call he had received during the court's proceedings. It had been the managing partner of his firm, Michelle Bennett, calling him in a panic to inform him that his former client, Mr. Park, had been found murdered. At that moment, Ethan had brushed it aside as unimportant, but it dawned on him now that this made Liam his fourth client who had been murdered in the past three years. Why were his clients dying after he won their cases for them?

Ethan's thoughts were interrupted as he heard Martin inquiring about his wound. He replied, "Yea, I'm fine now." He couldn't care less about himself right then.

His mind was racing, desperately trying to make some sense of what was happening. Then it struck him. 'How could I have been so blind?' he thought. He felt devastated as he realized what was happening.

"The insurance money. The millions of dollars!" he exclaimed.

All his past three dead clients were beneficiaries to large sums of insurance money, and so was Liam Montcherry.

He collapsed, cradling his head in his hands as some dreadful thoughts cropped up in his mind, 'What if someone connects the dots? His reputation of years could be destroyed! Who could be murdering his clients?'

Ethan's heart was racing, and his palms were sweating.

* * *

A Few Hours Prior

Liam had felt ecstatic on being acquitted. His not-so-perfect plan had worked. He had been desperately waiting to get hold of the insurance money and his freedom to gamble. Finally, today, after weeks and tons of paperwork, the bank did hand over the 10 million in cash he had asked for. He grinned as he thought of how he had been able to dupe the authorities by submitting papers for agro-trading, stating that his company wanted to diversify and needed large sums of cash to deal with farmers. He had asked his legal team to do the necessary paperwork well in advance so that there would be no unnecessary hurdles after his acquittal. He had also made arrangements with his friend, Elijah

Taylor, the investment banker, to have the insurance money transferred to him without further delays. Elijah had found his interaction with Liam very suspicious, but since the court had acquitted him, he decided to believe in his friend. However, Liam didn't let anyone get a whiff of his actual plan. He was packing his bags to flee the country and go to Mexico.

Montcherry Luxury was on the verge of bankruptcy, and he had been stalling his vendors and staff regarding payments for quite some time. All his assets had been mortgaged as well. He smirked when he thought about how he had tampered with his financial statements and fooled Ethan into thinking that the company was capable of paying its debts, and that there were enough assets. However, in reality, he did not want to lose his hard-earned money to pay his debts and legal fees.

Ethan working alone and not trusting his associates for important work had backfired on him. He had not got Liam's financial records that were submitted to him double-checked.

Liam could not wait to gamble after he had got his hands on the cash. His addiction had taken over his sense of reasoning. All he could think about was gambling, and Mexico seemed like a safe place to him. Though he could afford a chartered flight to Mexico, he chose to flee under disguise in a train and then by road to enter Mexico, so as to not raise suspicion and disappear without leaving any trace. Once in Mexico, Liam would be untouchable due to his contacts there.

He couldn't help marveling at the brilliant execution

of his plan. At the back of his mind, he recollected the events that had compelled him to take such a step on that fateful night.

The nagging question still remained unanswered, "WHO. KILLED. LIAM?"

Chapter 17

The Montcherry Marriage

Six Months into the Marriage

Liam had got hopelessly addicted to gambling. It had started with a trip to Vegas where he won a large amount in the game of blackjack. Trouble began when he insisted on going there the next weekend as well, only this time he lost a lot of money. He started gambling almost every day thereafter. He kept believing that he would cover his losses in the next game, but it never happened. Soon, he was so addicted that his sense of reasoning went down the drain. He made bad choices and continued playing high stakes, relying on pure luck. Cloe had started becoming a problem for him, as she kept forcing him to stop gambling. She began keeping a close tab on all his expenses to help him out of his addiction. She also threatened to file for divorce and sue him for his gambling losses, as it was company money that had collaboration with her brand.

This pushed Liam to look at other avenues to make some money for gambling. He believed his wife was foolish to not allow him to cover his losses with just another round of gambling. His pride did not allow him to ask his friends for money. The desperation to arrange for some money grew over the months. Then, one evening, while watching a murder mystery movie, it struck him.

Right after their marriage, Liam's close friend, Elijah Taylor, who was a financial consultant in a leading firm, had called him. Elijah told him about his company's life insurance policy. He had explained to Liam the need of having a life insurance policy and how important it was for every household. Since Elijah was standing at a deadline, he was ready to give Liam some added benefits, like lower annual premiums. Liam had agreed and taken 50-million-dollar life insurance policies for both of them.

The movie planted the idea of availing the benefits of the insurance policy. There was, unfortunately, only one way to do it: get rid of his wife to claim the insurance amount. Since Cloe was keeping a close watch on his expenses, this plan would also help him gamble freely, he had thought.

Liam was an addict, not a killer. He cried for days for even having the thought of killing his wife for freedom, but at the back of his mind, he also wanted to open the track of getting gambling money through the insurance policy. Soon, Liam's mind was filled with greed, and he started to plan the best way to get the money in his name and absolute freedom to gamble without anyone finding out. He decided on hiring someone to kill his wife, Cloe, as he could never kill even a fly, let alone his wife. His mother-in-law was the only person in the family who knew of the policy and could be a problem. However, he was aware of her mental health condition that was leading to memory loss and hallucinations. He hoped that she would either forget about it, or that no one would believe her due to her mental state.

He then started to look for trusted people whom he could pay to kill, but hit a dead-end. He was an industrialist, not part of some mafia, to be able to easily connect with contract killers. Soon, he realized that he would have to do the job himself.

To be able to find a scapegoat, he began digging into Cloe's past. He checked the social media accounts of all of Cloe's friends, but didn't find anything useful. He then checked the accounts of all her old friends' friends. That was a humongous exercise and a painful one. Liam kept himself motivated to keep going by reminding himself of being able to play once again to his heart's content at the casinos in Vegas. One of Cloe's friends' friends had a picture of Cloe with him on one of his posts. The man seemed to be oddly familiar. When he checked the 'about' section of his account, he realized that he was the head chef at his favorite restaurant. While going through some more posts on the chef's social media page, he discovered that the chef had been dating his wife years back. Liam beamed, as he had found the perfect person to frame as the killer.

Liam then went about meticulously planning the murder. He got a burner phone to read up about various types of poison on the internet. The burner phone did not leave a trace and worked perfectly for him, as he did not want this search showing up in his browsing history. He eventually identified and sourced the poison to murder his wife. He hired a trustworthy professional hacker, who went by the name, Diamond, on the dark web, to teach him how to enable and disable CCTV cameras remotely without leaving a trace. This was an essential skill he needed to have as he did not want the CCTV cameras at his home catching anything suspicious; too much was at stake.

Liam planned the anniversary dinner at the same restaurant where this chef worked. Upon entering the restaurant, he informed the lady at the reception that they were celebrating their first anniversary. He knew it was standard practice at the restaurant for the head chef to come and honor the guests on special occasions. Over the years, he had seen the chef many times, sometimes at other tables and sometimes at his.

Liam made sure the CCTV cameras of the restaurant caught their complete interaction there.

He was all set for his next round of gambling; all he had to do was poison his wife's drink that night.

The Night of the Murder

Liam had arranged for some soothing green tea at home after they returned from their anniversary dinner. The CCTV cameras had been disabled and the staff had been dismissed early, giving him all the privacy he needed. This green tea was the dreadful poisoned tea that Liam had sourced for Cloe; it was his ticket to uninterrupted gambling and end of life for his once beloved.

As Liam poured the tea and stirred the poison into the cup for his trusting wife, his eyes filled up with tears. He used to be a good man, but he was now possessed by addiction.

He quickly pocketed the empty poison bottle and served the cup to Cloe.

As Liam observed his wife sipping the tea, a part of him wished he could snap out of it and live a simple happy life with Cloe. Unfortunately, his addiction was stronger than his good sense.

Cloe enjoyed her tea while Liam bid her a silent goodbye.

Soon after, Cloe slept. When Liam had checked on the internet, he had read that the poison would take effect between one and four hours from consuming. This had kept Cloe's drink at the restaurant within the time window. He had figured out that Cloe would die in her sleep. His friend called unexpectedly that night to invite him over to his place. Liam agreed as he thought it would give him an alibi for the night and went to his friend's place. He watched Cloe sleeping peacefully and felt immense guilt. He planned to get rid of the empty poison bottle on his way and carried it in his jacket pocket.

As he sat at his friend's place, he started feeling like he couldn't rely on the poison completely. This was his first time dealing with any kind of poison. He preferred his earlier plan of having been around to make sure everything worked well. Suddenly, he realized that he had forgotten his phone at home. He then cursed himself for leaving his house on this crucial night. He wanted to go back home, but at the same time did not want to raise any suspicion. Just then, he got the perfect opportunity as his friends wanted to have pizza. He promptly offered to get it for them. On his way for the pizza, he stopped at his house for a peep. But when he entered his room, he panicked to see Cloe gasping for breath and frantically trying to dial someone.

When she saw Liam standing there, she looked relieved and said while panting, "Li... Liam, I... I'm feeling unwell. I was trying to call mom as y... You had left your phone here."

Liam panicked and blurted, "You are still alive!!" and ran towards her with a pillow, trying to suffocate her.

Cloe was utterly shocked as she realized that Liam was trying to kill her. With whatever little strength she had, she tried to fend for herself. In the struggle, she attempted to dial 911, but Liam smashed her phone. The call got disconnected before even going through. Just then, Cloe collapsed on the floor and stopped moving. Liam checked her pulse; she was dead.

He was now sweating profusely, as he had not planned to kill his wife in this manner. His alibi was breaking up with the added time he had spent here. He quickly cleared all signs of struggle in the room and placed his wife on the bed, as if she was sleeping. Just as he was about to leave, he noticed the broken phone by the bedside. He decided he had to now make it appear like a break-in to be able to explain the broken phone. His mind had stopped working. In a state of panic, he left a pillow on her face to depict a struggle and ran out, closing the door behind him.

Had he thought logically, he would have at least left some signs of a struggle and broken the door or a window to show a break-in. He realized that he had again left his phone behind. He shrugged, but then thought that it was a good thing to have happened. There was a chance that his friends would have noticed him without a phone before his trip for the pizza.

Liam froze as he felt the poison bottle in his pocket when he was searching for his car keys. He couldn't think of a place to get rid of it at. He was already late with the pizza and couldn't afford to spare any more time. He decided to keep it on him till he figured out a place to discard it safely. His heart was racing, and he was in no condition to meet his friends back at the house without raising suspicion. He sat in his car and calmed himself down to clear his head. He suddenly thought of the professional hacker, Diamond, who had the reputation of being the best hacker on the dark web. Liam called him up in desperation through his burner phone and promised him a heavy bribe in exchange for deleting the footage of him going from Davis's house to his own house, and then from his own house to the gas station from the public CCTV cameras. Liam breathed a sigh of relief as he agreed. At the time, he could not think of a better way to cover his tracks. He then quickly broke the burner phone and got rid of it. He decided to fill the gap in his pizza-run alibi by inventing a fictitious story about a man who wanted to be dropped off at the station. He tried to be his usual jovial self and went back with the pizza. However, his friends did not seem to have noticed the extra time he took, so he avoided narrating the made-up story to them. Liam felt relieved.

While he tried to act as normal as possible with his friends all night, he was also mentally preparing himself to accept that he had killed his wife.

By the time Liam left for home early that morning, he was ready to mourn the death of his wife.

Chapter 18
The Ultimate Conspiracy

Two Hours Prior to Ethan's Arrival at Liam's House

Liam had got custom secret compartments made in his bags to hide the bundles of cash. He wanted a safe and uneventful travel to Mexico with the cash. As he packed his belongings, he felt proud for having got the cash without any hitches. He had also got the balance amount of the insurance money transferred into his offshore bank accounts in the Bahamas. Once he disappeared, there would be no way to catch him or his money.

Liam valued his house help dearly. He had paid their dues with an additional two-months' salary to help them during the time they find a new job. He made sure that his staff left his property before he fled so they don't get caught up in his mess afterwards. He had also made sure to lock the outhouse after they left.

Liam was a good man, but addiction had

destroyed the peace in his life. He smiled with glee at the thought of gambling at the casinos without Cloe hovering over him.

Meanwhile, a shadow moved slightly behind the curtain. A man had been watching him from behind. He was wearing a black hoodie, and his face could not be seen. Normally, he was an impatient man, but today, he watched with patience as Liam packed.

The man was waiting in silence for the perfect opportunity to steal the cash without harming Liam. He had planned for this day months in advance. He had identified the window to break to be able to enter the house quietly, but had been surprised when he was welcomed by so many open windows. 'Liam sure feels safe in his house,' he had thought to himself and had smirked while jumping in through one of the open windows. He was relieved when he heard in court that the CCTV cameras in and around Liam's house were not working, as it gave him one less job to do.

Liam zipped up his bags full of cash and went to the bathroom. The only thing remaining to be done before he left was to take the empty poison bottle from his jacket in the attic. This was the man's perfect opportunity as he saw Liam's bags unattended. He quickly stepped forward and started emptying all the secret compartments of the bag and filling his own bag with the cash. Just then, the man accidentally dropped a bundle of cash, which made the slightest sound. Normally, such a faint sound would be ignored, but when millions of dollars are lying open in the house, the slightest sound becomes the loudest alarm. Liam was startled and shouted from the bathroom, "Who's there?!!" The man looked back hastily.

There was no way the man could empty all the secret compartments and disappear with the cash before Liam came out of the bathroom. He had no choice but to confront Liam if he had to leave with the 10 million dollars. The man took out his gun and pointed it at the closed bathroom door, preparing himself to commit one more murder, even though he had tried his best to avoid it this time. As soon as Liam opened the bathroom door to exit, the man shot at him. In the blink of an eye, Liam collapsed on the floor. The man felt guilty, but decided that it wasn't worth the risk to stay and call the ambulance. He knew he had run, and fast. He left Liam lying on the bathroom floor, shut the door partially in a rush, and quickly filled his bag with the cash.

Before he left, he decided to make it look like a break-in and trashed the room. He smashed the table glass near the sofa, pulled out things from cupboards and broke some furniture. He was about to break the main door and furniture in the living room when he heard a car pulling in. He realized he had no more time to make it look like a break-in. He now wanted to avoid drawing anyone's attention to the trashed room, as Liam's body was in the bathroom attached to this room. He quickly switched off the lights in the room and ran out towards the back exit. As he was running out, he saw Ethan and his associate pull into the building. He felt trapped and nervously hid under a table near the exit door. The man wondered if he should have simply shot Liam and fled with the cash. Trying to steal the money while keeping Liam alive had landed him in this mess. He couldn't believe he was hiding under a table. After what seemed like an eternity to the man, there was a sudden thud in the house followed by silence. It was the sound made by Ethan's fall near Liam's body. The man took the opportunity and stealthily crept out of the house and into the garden.

The shadow lurked in the bushes. Desperately trying to hide the murder weapon, the gun, was Ethan's most trusted friend, Timothy.

The last three times, he was unable to take the money without killing. This time, he had planned to steal the readily available cash from Liam and flee without killing him. Unfortunately, things did not go as per his plan.

He targeted Ethan's wealthy clients who won insurance claims, as the sudden influx of liquid money was easier to extort. As he was the medical advisor to Ethan and had free access to Ethan's office due to their friendship, he had insider details of cases at his disposal. He made several lunch and drinks plans with Ethan regularly during trials and made sure to arrive early at his office to pick him, to be able to eavesdrop on case conversations. He would then use means to dig into the clients' past, use the information against them to blackmail them, and force them to pay up. It was easy for Timothy to pick his target as he was sure that all of his clients would definitely get acquitted, owing to Ethan's fabulous skills.

When he felt he had cashed the clients out

completely, he was compelled to kill them. He couldn't risk them going to the cops or getting him killed.

The extortion money was either taken in cash or transferred to his accounts that had been set up for this very purpose in Seychelles. Timothy would then pass the money to his ex-partner, who had been blackmailing him for years.

A CCTV camera footage of Timothy accidentally murdering a business tycoon years ago was like a noose around his neck. His ex-partner from the drug business had possession of it and was constantly blackmailing him for money. His dark past had caught up with him even after his acquittal from the drug case that Ethan had got him out of. The ex-partner had asked for a smaller amount the first time, which Timothy had managed to pay very quickly as he was doing well in the medical field. He then got greedy and threw a large figure at Timothy that was impossible for him to get with his medical income.

Timothy was left with no option but to take the law in his hands. That venomous mind of his reared up as he came up with a plan to kill two birds with one stone.

He then found the route of easy money by blackmailing Ethan's clients for it. As a ripple effect, it would tarnish Ethan's image, as one by one his clients would get robbed. He would no longer be considered as the number one person in his field. He would also lose self-respect for having failed so miserably and being responsible for the deaths of his clients.

Timothy's own success meant little to him. His heart

burned with jealousy whenever he met Ethan, though he managed to hide it exceptionally well. Both had grown up in the same environment. Yet Ethan had managed to become the best and most respected attorney in the country, while Timothy had to be rescued by Ethan, who had taken pity on him and got him acquitted in the drug case.

At last, it seemed as if he had attained both his goals. These 10 million dollars were the last of the payments he had to make to his ex-partner. He would get the CCTV recording of his crime and would be free from the blackmailing. Timothy had also managed to get back at Ethan, for achieving all the glory that he could never get. Eventually, someone would be able to connect the dots, and Ethan would be finished.

He had the last laugh, and his eyes shone with malice as he executed one of the most well-planned crimes ever.

THE END